Serendipity: A Chain of Impossible Coincidences

OrangeBooks Publication

1st Floor, Rajhans Arcade, Mall Road, Kohka, Bhilai, Chhattisgarh 490020
Website: **www.orangebooks.in**

First Edition, 2025

ISBN: 978-93-6554-488-6

Price: Rs. 216.00

Printed in India

Serendipity: A Chain of Impossible Coincidences

When the Universe Writes Better Stories Than We Do

Balesh Lakshminarayanan

OrangeBooks Publication
www.orangebooks.in

Dedication

To my family —

To Aiswarya, my partner in every story, whose quiet strength and unwavering belief in me have been my anchor through every chapter of life.

To Adhrit, whose laughter reminds me that life's most beautiful moments are often unplanned.

And most of all, to Avyukt — the little spark who reignited the reader in me, one bedtime book at a time. Your insatiable curiosity, endless questions, and love for stories made me fall in love with reading all over again... and eventually led me to write this one.

This book is yours as much as it is mine.

Preface

This book wasn't planned. It wasn't outlined on a whiteboard or tucked away in a dusty notebook waiting for its turn. It was born—serendipitously—out of stillness, silence, and a sudden pause in life.

A few months ago, I found myself stuck at home for an extended period. Due to the risk of infection, my mobility was severely restricted. For someone used to travelling, building, mentoring, and moving at full throttle, it felt like life had yanked the brakes hard.

In that unexpected stillness, I wrote a story—just one—on a whim. I wasn't trying to write a book. I just needed to tell a tale. That little story meandered its way to a few friends. They laughed, they paused, and a few even said, "That felt like something bigger." And before I knew it, I was writing another. And then another.

Most of these stories are pieced together from years of wandering, wondering, and wide-eyed watching across airports and alleyways, conference rooms and cafés. They're inspired by real people, half-remembered conversations, books that lingered, and animes that whispered, *"What if?"*

Of course, none of this would've been possible without technology. Tools like GPT helped me turn scattered thoughts into structured stories, refine rough scenes, and spark new ideas when my creative tank was low.

What you now hold is a collection of bite-sized, serendipitous adventures—the book designed to be read in a single sitting, maybe over a two-hour flight or a rainy afternoon. It's not meant to be literary or lofty. It's meant to feel like a story a friend might tell you on a long drive, with a laugh, a twist, and a quiet "huh or hmmm" at the end.

In many ways, this book is my little serendipity. I hope it finds you at the right moment—and maybe becomes yours too.

~ ***Balesh Lakshminarayanan***

Disclaimer

This is a work of fiction. All characters, events, institutions, and scenarios depicted in this book are products of the author's imagination or are used in a fictitious manner for the purpose of storytelling. Any resemblance to actual persons, living or dead, or to actual events, locales, or organisations is purely coincidental.

The stories in this anthology span multiple genres—historical reimagining's, speculative fiction, magical realism, satire, and science fiction. While some stories may draw inspiration from mythology, current affairs, or scientific concepts, they are artistic interpretations and not intended as factual commentary, historical analysis, or scientific documentation.

The author does not intend to mock, misrepresent, or defame any religion, culture, institution, or individual. Any cultural references, mythological figures, or belief systems mentioned herein are done with respect and creative liberty. The reinterpretation of sacred texts or historical epics is purely fictional and should not be construed as scholarly or theological viewpoints.

Some content may include surreal coincidences, unexplained phenomena, or extraordinary events presented for entertainment and philosophical reflection.

Readers are encouraged to enjoy the stories as imaginative what-ifs rather than predictive truths.

If any reader identifies unintended inaccuracies or wishes to offer feedback, the author welcomes constructive dialogue and values diverse perspectives.

Contents

Chapter - 1
The One-Legged Guard

In the heart of Jaipur, when camels still roamed the pink sandstone streets and the scent of jasmine floated through the palace courtyards, lived Bhairav Singh — a palace guard with a crooked smile, a weathered spear, and an undying sense of duty.

Bhairav was not the strongest, nor the fastest among the guards. His arms lacked the sculpted definition of a seasoned warrior, and his swordplay was, at best, modest. Yet, he was the first to arrive at the palace gates and the last to leave. His humble devotion earned him a little respect among his peers, who often mocked him behind his back.

At home, Bhairav's world was a far sweeter place. His wife, Meera, a woman with a laugh as bright as morning light, often teased him, "You may not scare the invaders, but you've certainly conquered my heart." Their two children, Arjun and Gauri, thought of their father as nothing less than a hero. And in truth, Bhairav was rich in all the ways that counted.

The king, Maharaja Veerendra Singh, was a man wise beyond his years. He saw through Bhairav's awkwardness and recognised a rare jewel: honesty unmarred by ambition. While other guards flaunted bravado, Bhairav listened, observed, and spoke when needed — and always with sincerity. It was no surprise to the palace servants when the king would sometimes pause during his grand marches just to exchange a few words with Bhairav.

Queen Rani Devika, however, was less sentimental. "You trust too easily, Veerendra," she would chide over evening meals. "One day, it may cost you more than you know."

One monsoon afternoon, when the air was thick and the peacocks silent, the king set out on a hunting expedition to the deep jungles. Bhairav, ever eager to serve, insisted on joining, despite the jeers of fellow guards.

Unknown to many, whispers had begun to rise in the deserts beyond — whispers of betrayal. The neighbouring kingdom of Malwa had grown restless. Discreet messengers, disguised as traders and scholars, infiltrated Jaipur, quietly sowing discontent. A few guards had been compromised — their loyalties bought with coin and promise.

It was during this fateful journey, with the cicadas singing and mist wrapping the trees like cotton, that disaster struck. As the party moved through a narrow trail, a massive bear — its fur matted and eyes wild — lunged from the thickets. The king's horse reared, throwing him into the mud.

Chaos ensued. Arrows flew wide. Spears clattered to the ground. But Bhairav, without hesitation, threw himself between the beast and the king. He jabbed with his spear, feeble against the bear’s rage. The bear swiped, ripping through Bhairav's leg like paper. Yet somehow, with a final desperate thrust, Bhairav diverted the bear long enough for others to rally and bring it down.

Bhairav woke three days later, his right leg gone. Meera sat beside him, smiling through her tears. "A lost leg is a small price for a saved life," she said, cupping his roughened hand.

The King, deeply moved, ordered the finest artisans to craft a wooden leg for him, carved from sacred sandalwood, polished with oils from the royal garden. It fit perfectly. Functionally, it worked. Emotionally, it hurt.

Meera said, "You were meant for something greater, Bhairav." True to her words, the king awarded Bhairav the Medal of Honour and named him Chief Sentinel of the Royal Chambers — an elite position once reserved for the strongest warriors. The announcement sent murmurs through the barracks. Many guards bristled with resentment, their pride wounded by the elevation of a "cripple."

Queen Devika confronted the king. "Why trust a man who cannot even chase an intruder?" she asked.

King Veerendra smiled calmly. "My Queen, there are many who can run fast and strike hard. But few will throw away their life without a thought. Loyalty is faster than any foot, and sharper than any sword."

The Queen shook her head but said no more.

Bhairav now stood outside the Queen's chambers nightly. Some saluted him with respect. Some sneered behind his back.

Only Meera understood.

Every evening, she would kneel by his wooden foot, polish it gently, and say, “Even this has a purpose. One day, this wood will do what flesh could not.”

He didn’t always believe her. The foot, though skilfully made, felt alien. He’d often stare at it, thinking about what was lost — and what almost was.

Yet fate, that mischievous weaver of ironies, was not done.

Across the border, in the rival kingdom of Malwa, enemies plotted. It was they who had released the bear, though none at court suspected it. Their failure only emboldened them.

Weeks later, in the stillness of a starless night, they found a subtler way. A royal assassin slipped into the palace gardens and released a king cobra into the royal bedchamber, coiled and silent beneath the silken sheets.

It was Rani Devika who first saw it, its eyes twin embers in the candlelight. She froze, her heart thundering in her chest. One wrong movement, and death would strike.

The palace guards, summoned in hushed panic, stood at the threshold, paralysed. None dared approach. A king cobra's bite was swift, sure, and lethal.

And then, a shuffle.

Bhairav, with his wooden leg thumping softly against marble, entered the room. Without a word, he grabbed a cloth, approached slowly, and with a precision born not of training but of pure stillness of spirit, threw the cloth over the snake.

The snake struck once, twice. But Bhairav did not flinch.

He didn't draw a weapon. He didn't call for help.

He stomped.

The cobra hissed. It rose.

And struck.

Fangs pierced lacquered wood.

The cobra recoiled, its venom wasted. In that moment of distraction, Bhairav used the blunt end of his spear to pin it. With a sharp motion, he flipped it into a basket, and in one fluid movement, Bhairav scooped the creature up and contained it.

The Queen, tears in her eyes, whispered, "You have saved me, Bhairav."

Later, as Bhairav sat alone under the neem tree outside the palace, he smiled to himself. He remembered Meera's words, spoken long ago, cradling his bandaged stump: *"Every fall is the beginning of a climb you cannot yet see."*

In a way only destiny could explain, the leg he lost to save a king saved a queen.

Sometimes, Bhairav mused, life stitched its greatest patterns from the most frayed threads.

"Serendipity weaves through humble lives,
unseen until the day it saves a kingdom."

Chapter - 2
The Whisper of The Vineyard

I was born under a forgiving sun, in a valley tucked away between the rolling meadows of Tuscany. From the first breath of morning dew to the long, golden afternoons, my world was a tapestry of soft breezes, scattered daisies, and the distant hum of life from the grand château on the hill.

The vineyard was a sacred place, a kingdom ruled by careful hands and knowing eyes. My siblings, those plump, proud grapes, were nurtured with love, whispered to by the vineyard keepers, caressed by the mist. I, however, was an accident — a stubborn sprout from an abandoned vine near the old stone wall.

Nobody paid me much attention. Not the Master Winemaker, Signore Bartolomeo, whose nose could detect a summer rain in a barrel of oak. Nor the strong vineyard boys who pruned and watered the chosen ones. I clung to life on the edge of the world, unseen but wildly alive.

Seasons danced past me. I grew under the jealous gaze of the sun, shivering in the tender rains, swaying when the mistral winds came to gossip over the hills. The earth fed me with forgotten kindness.

One day, a giggle broke the monotony. A little girl with fiery curls — Lucia — wandered away from the château gardens. She wore a linen dress and muddy boots. Her hands, soft and curious, found me. She brushed away the weeds and tilted her head. "Papa says you're no good," she whispered. "But Nonno says treasure sometimes grows where no one looks."

I became her secret.

When autumn arrived, the world turned into a carnival of colour. The vineyard bustled with harvesters. Songs floated on the crisp air. Crates filled with the proud grapes destined for barrels and bottles bound for kings.

And me? Lucia plucked me gently, along with my awkward siblings, and tossed us into a small basket she carried herself. Under the watchful eyes of her disapproving father and the twinkling grin of her grandfather, she stomped us in a little oak vat. Her feet were clumsy, her laughter infectious. My world collapsed into a dark, rich swirl.

Crushed, pulped, and pressed into a humble bottle, I found myself corked and forgotten in the attic of the château, among broken chairs, moth-eaten drapes, and dreams packed away.

Years stretched long like shadows at dusk.

Through the dusty green glass of my bottle, I glimpsed the world. Turbulent times swept through the valley. Soldiers marched down dirt roads. Distant fires painted the horizon crimson. Walls shook under the rumble of iron beasts.

Vineyards were trampled, families scattered. Yet somehow, high in the forgotten attic, I endured.

One day, a wandering man in a tattered uniform stumbled upon me. His hands were rough but reverent. He marvelled at my dusty bottle, tucked me into his battered sack, and carried me far from home. But he never opened me. I became a relic of a memory too fragile to uncork.

I slept again, tucked away in a trunk, hidden in a seaside cottage where salt clung to the air and rosemary bloomed wild. Decades drifted by, as unnoticed and patient as the tides.

Then, fate stirred.

Without warning, I found myself in the glittering halls of a renowned auction house. Under the eyes of velvet-draped patrons and flashing cameras, I was placed carefully under a crystal dome. The auctioneer's gavel gleamed. Whispers filled the air.

"An unknown vintage."

"A mysterious sigil."

"A story waiting to be told."

No one knew my full origins, but that mystery became my greatest charm. Bidders waved their paddles with mounting excitement. The numbers climbed, faster and faster, until the final gavel struck. I had become the most talked-about bottle in the world overnight.

The sigil on my worn label, faint but defiant, captured imaginations. Scholars and sommeliers speculated endlessly. Theories brewed like heady perfumes, but none knew the truth.

It took five more years for the real discovery to unfold.

A teenage girl, fiery-haired like Lucia once was, posted a photograph online — a rustic Halloween display at her family's old farm, filled with vintage barrels and faded vineyard stamps. Among the dusty relics, the same sigil shimmered in the sunlight.

An eagle-eyed sommelier browsing late-night forums spotted the post. The buzz reignited. Wine historians traced the farm back to a sleepy, almost forgotten vineyard in Tuscany.

And there they found her — Lucia, now silver-haired and stoop-shouldered, standing among stubborn vines still singing their quiet song. Her laughter, weathered but bright, echoed the same spirit that had once plucked a lonely grape from a forgotten vine.

The vineyard, once gasping for survival, bloomed anew. Crowds came to walk the paths where fate had hidden its greatest treasure. Old debts were forgiven. New vines sprang up, strong and sure.

And I — I rest now behind a pane of glass, basking in sunlight, cradled in velvet, a simple grape that dared to believe in the sun, the rain, and the small, stubborn love of a little girl.

"Sometimes, the greatest vintages are born not in crafted perfection, but in forgotten corners of the world, kissed only by accident and kindness."

Chapter - 3
The God Outside the Temple

Tucked between the lush paddy fields and ancient temple corridors of Palakkad, where the border winds carry the whispers of Kerala and Tamil Nadu alike, lived Maya.

Palakkad was a land caught in the gentle clutch of time. Grand agraharams, with their sloping tiled roofs and sunlit courtyards, stood beside sprawling banyan trees and murmuring canals. The air smelled of wet earth, jasmine, and the faint scent of camphor from the countless temples. Generations of Tamil Iyers had settled here, long before Tipu Sultan's horses thundered through these passes, leaving behind stories etched in every stone.

In this sleepy village, Maya lived a life that was simple but never easy. Her days began with the rising sun; the rhythmic clang of the temple bells her first call to duty. She swept the modest courtyard, helped Amma string fragrant garlands for the temple deity, bathed her little brothers, and then rushed to school, clutching second-hand books in a frayed cloth bag.

Maya's father, a kind-hearted priest, had passed away when she was just eight. Since then, life had been a careful balancing act. Yet amid the humble bustle, Maya nurtured a singular, audacious dream: to crack the NEET exam and become a doctor.

Every evening, while the other children played in the fading light, Maya could be found at the temple's side hall, her nose buried in textbooks. The temple, with its unwavering generator light, was her refuge against the frequent power cuts that left the village swathed in darkness.

It was here that she first saw him.

"Swamy Uncle," as Maya came to call him, was an enigma. Draped in a simple veshti, a towel slung carelessly over his shoulder, he would appear suddenly, always in a hurry, muttering to himself or smiling softly at no one in particular. No one knew where he came from or where he vanished to. Some said he was an ascetic, others a madman, others a ghost from an older world.

But for Maya, he was God.

Their first meeting was etched in her memory. She had been deep in study when she heard a shriek. Her youngest brother, Krishna, was dangling precariously from the temple chariot — an ancient, dust-laden structure that was pulled out only once a year for the festival. Despite her warnings, his mischievous spirit had gotten the better of him.

Maya watched, horror-struck, as Krishna fell with a thud, his arm twisted grotesquely. Before the panic could fully take hold, Swamy Uncle was there. Calmly, he knelt, tore the towel from his waist, fashioned a sling, and with a quick, deft manoeuvre, reset the dislocated shoulder. A sharp cry from Krishna, a "click," and it was done.

Maya had witnessed magic. Or so she thought.

From that day onward, whenever she spotted Swamy Uncle, she would run to him with questions, stories, and shy smiles. One evening, as they sat on the temple steps, he chuckled and told her, "I learned that trick from a great doctor I once knew."

Maya's eyes widened with wonder. "I want to be like him! I want to be a doctor!" she declared.

Swamy Uncle laughed, a deep, knowing laugh that echoed through the stone pillars. "Then you must study ten times harder, little one."

Perhaps moved by something in her determined gaze, Swamy Uncle began bringing her books. Old, precious textbooks, worn at the edges but filled with wisdom. Each book carried careful underlines, margin notes, and markings — crisp, simple explanations that made even the toughest concepts easy to understand. Maya often felt that these notes were her greatest treasure, like whispered secrets handed down directly from the gods.

He would pass them casually during his visits, always claiming, "My doctor friend says this book is good for you. Read this topic. Practice that chapter."

Curiously, whatever he suggested often seemed to appear in Maya's exams. It only deepened her conviction that he was sent by the gods themselves.

Years rolled on. Maya grew taller, leaner, her spirit harder, but her eyes no less bright. As her NEET exam approached, her anxiety knotted her stomach. It had been months since she had seen Swamy Uncle. She longed for his reassuring smile, his quiet nod of belief.

The night before her exam, Maya sat by the temple pond, sleepless, the cool breeze offering little comfort. She whispered a prayer into the starlit sky, "Please, just one more time."

Morning broke. Maya entered the exam hall, her heart hammering against her ribs. Her hands trembled as she checked her roll number and settled into her seat.

And then, through the glass corridor, she thought she saw him — Swamy Uncle, in his simple veshti, walking past with a serene smile and a slow nod, his eyes twinkling with pride.

Maya's fear melted away. Her mind sharpened. Her pen moved with certainty.

Months later, clad in a crisp white salwar, Maya stood at the threshold of her new life — her first day at the prestigious medical college. As the orientation ceremony began, the announcer's voice echoed through the grand hall:

"Ladies and gentlemen, please welcome our Dean, Dr. Swaminathan."

Maya turned, breath caught in her chest, as Dr. Swaminathan — Swamy Uncle himself — walked onto the stage. His eyes found hers in the crowd, and he gave the same smile, the same proud nod.

Her God had not only guided her path. He had been waiting at its summit.

"Sometimes, the simplest faith, placed in unseen hands, lifts us to heights we dare not imagine."

Chapter - 4
The Lucky Ghost of Sakura Alley

The sky above Sakura Alley was a swirl of pink and gold, the cherry blossoms shedding their final petals like a slow, delicate rain. Children, barely tall enough to reach the low-hanging branches, sat in a loose circle, eyes wide and sparkling. In their midst, hunched on a low wooden stool, sat Grandpa Taro — the village storyteller, the keeper of old secrets.

"Tell us about Kenta again!" shouted little Hiro, waving his arms in excitement.

Grandpa Taro chuckled, his breath misting in the cool evening air. "Ah, Kenta... the ghost who could never quite get it right."

The children squealed in delight. They loved the tales of Kenta, the mischievous but harmless spirit said to have once saved Sakura Alley.

Grandpa Taro's eyes twinkled as he began. "You see, many years ago, when I was about your age, Sakura Alley was almost lost forever. They wanted to tear down our ramen stalls, our lanterns, even the old tea shop where your mothers and fathers had their first dates."

He leaned in conspiratorially. "But Kenta... Kenta had other plans."

The children giggled, nudging each other.

"Kenta was no ordinary ghost," Grandpa Taro said. "He wasn't scary. He tried to be, oh yes! He wailed, he made the wind blow, he rattled bamboo chimes at night. But instead of screams, he got laughter. Instead of fear, he got rice balls left out for him!"

The children roared with laughter.

"Once," Grandpa Taro continued, "he tried to scare a lovestruck couple by snapping the branch of the cherry tree they were standing under. He thought he'd make them run away! But instead, he shook the branch just enough that blossoms rained down on them... and they thought it was a blessing from the heavens!"

"Did they get married?" squeaked Emi, her pigtails bobbing.

"Of course!" Grandpa Taro said, winking. "Kenta accidentally started the tradition of 'Sakura Proposals' we have even today."

The children clapped and cheered.

Grandpa Taro leaned closer, lowering his voice to a dramatic whisper. "But there was one time... one very important time... when Kenta actually succeeded."

The children leaned in, wide-eyed.

"It was during the Great Lantern Festival many years ago. Sakura Alley was at its most beautiful, with paper lanterns floating in the sky like stars. But late that night, a group of bandits crept into the village, planning to steal everything — the temple treasures, the shopkeepers' earnings, even the children's festival gifts."

Gasps rose from the circle.

"The villagers were fast asleep, unaware of the danger. Only Kenta was awake, floating lazily through the alley. When he saw the bandits sneaking in, something inside him snapped! This was his home. His friends. His ramen!"

The children giggled.

"So, Kenta did what he did best... badly. He tried to wail— and instead knocked over a cart of festival drums, making a deafening racket! He tried to scare them with ghostly moans — and accidentally set off the leftover fireworks from the celebration!"

Grandpa Taro clapped his hands loudly, making the children jump.

"BOOM!" he shouted. "BANG! CRASH!"

"The bandits thought the gods themselves had woken up angry! They dropped everything and ran screaming into the night, never to be seen again."

The children roared with laughter and applause.

"And from that day," Grandpa Taro said, "no one dared lay a finger on Sakura Alley. All thanks to our very own, very clumsy, very lucky Kenta."

Grandpa Taro sighed contentedly, his gaze drifting beyond the children. If they looked carefully, they might have seen it too — the faint shimmer of a figure in a faded yukata, lounging lazily under the lanterns.

"Kenta," Grandpa Taro said under his breath, smiling, "one more time, for old times' sake?"

There was a sudden rustle in the air. A bamboo wind chime clanged wildly. A low, mournful wail floated across the alley. The children gasped, clutching each other.

"Whoooooo!" the voice moaned. The lanterns bobbed and spun. A pile of empty festival drums toppled with a satisfying crash.

Then — WHOOSH! With a flash, a hidden stash of fireworks shot into the sky, bursting in a shower of brilliant reds, blues, and golds. The alley lit up, the children's screams turning instantly into joyous squeals.

"Kenta!" they cried, dancing and twirling under the sparkling sky.

Grandpa Taro laughed so hard he had to wipe tears from his eyes. He tilted his head slightly, and for a moment — just a moment he could have sworn he saw Kenta grinning proudly beside him, adjusting an imaginary festival hat atop his translucent head.

"You always had a flair for the dramatic," Grandpa Taro whispered.

The fireworks faded, but the laughter lingered, curling into the night like incense smoke.

And in the heart of Sakura Alley, under the eternal cherry blossoms, the legend of the world's worst — and luckiest— ghost lived on.

"Sometimes, the ones who can't scare a soul end up stealing everyone's hearts."

Chapter - 5

The Journey of the Forgotten Toy

Long ago, in the grand halls of a small European kingdom, a toy unlike any other was crafted.

Smooth to the touch and warm as living skin, the toy was shaped like a delicate spinning top. No one could quite explain the origins of the metal, but it was said to have fallen from the heavens themselves.

The toy belonged to the young prince of the realm. In a palace filled with gold and jewels, it was this simple, spinning wonder that captured his heart. He would spend hours marvelling at how it spun endlessly on even the roughest surfaces, gleaming with an otherworldly shimmer.

As the centuries turned, kingdoms rose and fell. The spinning top changed hands - from royal heirs to noble guests, always cherished, always admired. Stories grew around it: some said it granted luck; others whispered it was a sign of divine favour.

But fortune is fickle.

During a great siege, as the royal family fled, the spinning top was hastily tossed into a river along with other treasures to prevent it from falling into enemy hands. Forgotten in the muddy currents, it lay buried in silt and time.

Years later, a fisherman casting nets in the misty river waters hauled up an enormous fish. As he gutted it, something clinked onto the worn wood of his boat - the spinning top, somehow gleaming as brightly as ever.

Believing it a gift from the river gods, the fisherman carried it to his village's humble church. There, the priest, entranced by its glow, declared it a holy relic. The top was placed near the altar, where villagers would light candles and whisper prayers beside it, believing it brought miracles.

Generations passed. The toy became a legend.

Eventually, scholars from distant cities arrived, curious about the "miraculous artefact." It was transported with great ceremony to a grand museum in the capital city. There, under glass and spotlights, the spinning top sat - nameless and timeless - catalogued as "The River Relic."

People came from far and wide to see it. Artists painted it. Poets wrote verses in their honour. It inspired dreams and superstitions in every heart it touched.

But progress is relentless.

As the modern world blossomed, technology advanced. Alloys stronger and lighter than anything before were created. Satellites soared, microchips shrank, and the wonders of the old world dimmed under neon lights.

One day, during a quiet renovation of the museum, an indifferent curator deemed the "River Relic" a curiosity of no scientific importance. Out of idle curiosity, he sent it for a materials analysis, where it was determined to be made of simple pewter - a once-precious alloy of tin and other metals, revered in olden days but rendered commonplace and overlooked in modern times.

No precious stones, no identifiable historical value, no technological marvel. Just an old toy.

Sold at auction for a pittance, the spinning top ended up at a dusty antique store, wedged between faded dolls and broken clocks.

A little girl wandering past the window one rainy afternoon spotted it. Her eyes lit up. With a few crumpled coins, she bought it and raced home.

And there, in the corner of a warm living room, on a simple wooden floor, the ancient toy spun once more, weaving circles of light and laughter as it had centuries ago - oblivious to its past, yet exactly where it was always meant to be.

"Not all treasures are measured by who remembers them, but by the joy they continue to bring."

Chapter - 6
The Ministry of Observation

Earth. Year 2150.

To the humans, the planet had never looked better. Towers of solar glass stretched through the clouds. Oceans shimmered with clean algae farms, and sky-rails zipped silently between cities with no wheels, no smoke, no delay. Drones hummed like mechanical bees, and the air was scented with cedar and ozone — a touch artificial, perhaps, but breathable.

To the alien known as Observant-Unit-4427, it still smelled like chaos.

Unit-4427 was not here on a whim. He was part of the Ministry of Observation, a wing of the Galactic Intelligence Council tasked with monitoring developing civilisations. Earth was a Level 7 species — smart enough to build machines, dumb enough to worship them.

He had last visited Earth when he was barely 200 orbital cycles old. A curious child in a strange galaxy, he'd left behind a small toy while hiding during a sandstorm in an Anatolian valley. His sister had cried about losing it all cycle-long.

Now, two thousand Earth years later, he was here to assess whether humans were finally ready for what the Ministry called "The Great Introduction."

His ship landed in stealth mode atop what had once been the Taurus Mountains. He and his fellow observer, Unit-1143, activated their anthropoid interface suits — human-like exos, complete with blinking eyes, bad knees, and surprisingly convincing Turkish accents.

Their first stop: Istanbul.

The Hagia Sophia still stood, albeit partially reconstructed with floating marble panels and anti-gravity scaffolding. As they walked among tourists from New Shanghai and Neo-Lagos, their human guide delivered a rehearsed speech filled with passion and post-colonial pride.

"So much history," 1143 whispered via sub-comm.

"Too much," 4427 muttered.

They stood before the dome that had seen emperors and sultans, crusaders and rebels, faiths born and unmade — all within these walls. The guide beamed, as if the blood etched into the stone was something to brag about.

They moved on to Göbekli Tepe — now an open-sky museum beneath a climate-controlled dome. The carvings were preserved, catalogued, and holographically reconstructed. An immersive AI let you experience the "first ritual feast" with realistic smells and dialogue based on excavated bone structure and dentition patterns.

Humans. Ever the romantics.

But 4427 felt something stir — a kind of nostalgia he couldn't quantify. Then came the final stop.

It was known as the Anatolian Relic Vault. Hidden in the vault's innermost chamber was what the guide breathlessly described as "the most fought-over object of the 22nd century."

"Recovered from the sands after the 4th Tech War. Once believed to be part of an ancient alien landing pod, it changed hands through five rebel governments, sparked two regional conflicts, and was the reason behind the Ankara Protocols of 2089," the guide declared, puffing his chest. "It is now the most visited artefact in the Eastern Hemisphere."

4427 narrowed his eyes.

They waited in a long queue, security scans buzzing over each visitor. Finally, they entered the chamber.

There, under shimmering light, surrounded by transparent force shields and ten motion-sensing drones… sat the artefact.

4427 stared.

It was a small purple object. Round. Bumpy. With tiny rotating arms and a faded label in Galactic Cyrillic that read: "Zoglup's Wobbleball™ — Now with Plasma Pops!"

His jaw dropped, though the exoskin hid it well.

"That's… that's my sister's toy," he whispered.

1143's eye ridges arched. "Are you certain?"

"She cried for hours when we left. She said Zoglup would never learn to wobble without her."

They stood in silence while the human guide continued, "Historians believe it symbolises duality — balance and chaos. The rotating arms were likely used for astral communication."

4427 nearly choked on his synthesised breath.

He spent the next thirty minutes listening to speculative nonsense, watching people take selfies and pledge devotion to a glorified squeaky ball.

Back aboard the ship, 4427 filed his report.

Civilisation Assessment: Earth – Level 7.3 Observational Summary: Advanced infrastructure and low-emission civilization. Partial AI symbiosis. Planetary peace sustained for 34 years. Cultural maturity: regressive. Artefact Significance Misattribution: Catastrophic. Recommendation: Postpone Galactic Introduction by 500 orbital cycles. Remarks: Still fighting over nonsense.

As the ship rose past the stratosphere, 4427 glanced at the blue planet below. Beautiful, bustling, brave — but still chasing shadows.

He shook his head and smiled. Somewhere, his sister would laugh herself silly.

"Sometimes, the wisest civilisations are the ones who know when to laugh at their past.
Earth isn't quite there yet."

Chapter - 7

The Seventh Car, Second Seat from the Right

It was a crisp spring morning in New York City, the kind that tricks you into thinking the city might be gentle for once. The E train rumbled its way uptown, shuddering under the weight of a million rushing thoughts.

In the seventh car, second seat from the right, sat Sister Agnes.

Her hands, worn but strong, held a small leather-bound diary filled with names — names of children she had raised in a sun-baked orphanage near Lake Turkana, northern Kenya. She had crossed the ocean on sheer faith and a grant from a local church, hoping to secure enough funds to keep the roof over their heads through the next monsoon season. She had chosen to take the subway that morning to save on taxi fare. But unfamiliar with the city's transit system, she kept nervously asking a fellow passenger about how many more stops to go, and how far she would have to walk.

Standing nearby, gripping a rail and balancing a coffee with a hint of despair, was David Carter. Twenty-nine, Detroit-born, Columbia Law graduate, and currently one misstep away from losing everything. His firm was representing a giant oil conglomerate fresh off a disastrous spill in Nigeria. His job? Make it go away. Or at least look like it never happened.

And this morning, he had one last shot to convince a humanitarian with global recognition to accept a multi-million-dollar donation as part of the company's CSR redemption tour. He hadn't seen a photo of the woman yet, but she was supposedly flying in from Nairobi. A regular subway commuter, David noticed the older woman's nervous chatter and noted the address she repeated several times.

Across from them sat Assemblywoman Linda Morales—sharp suit, sharper eyes, and a planner filled with campaign forecasts and pressure points. Born and bred in Queens, Linda had earned her stripes as a community organiser in the Bronx before clawing her way into the state legislature. Her next move: a public-private initiative connecting African humanitarian work to American corporate donors. She needed a big win. The kind that landed headlines and reelection.

Linda, however, was not having a normal morning. Her car had broken down just as she was leaving for the InterContinental. Begrudgingly, she had taken the subway— something she hadn't done in years. The crowds, the noise, the lack of control — all of it had frayed her mood. As she sat across from the suited young man who kept glancing around anxiously, she rolled her eyes inwardly. Probably fresh out of B-school, thinks the whole city owes him a seat.

And the nun? Kind eyes, but Linda wasn't in the mood for subway prayers.

Sister Agnes, for her part, watched them both. She could feel the anxiety radiating off the young man like subway heat. The woman had power — Agnes could always tell— but also carried invisible weights. Political ones, perhaps.

The train screeched to a halt at 53rd & Lexington. A tourist couple stumbled in. The nun gently helped the woman with her stroller. The train began to slow toward their stop.

As Sister Agnes stood, still unsure which direction to walk from the station, David looked up from his laptop.

"Excuse me, ma'am," he said, folding the screen shut. "You mentioned the Inter- Continental? I'm heading there too. I can walk with you."

She blinked, surprised. "Yes, I am. That would be most kind."

Linda watched the small moment unfold and raised an eyebrow. Maybe I misjudged that one, she thought. The gesture softened her mood.

With thirty minutes still to go before the meeting, she stepped out at the next station for a much-needed coffee.

Thirty minutes later, the boardroom on the 27th floor of the InterContinental buzzed with quiet anticipation. Executives, aides, consultants, and aides to the aides took their places.

David walked in, composed but tight-lipped, still rehearsing in his head. He was told the VIP guest was already inside. He hadn't been given her name.

Linda entered moments later, all business, now alert and caffeinated. She straightened her jacket and braced herself to pitch her vision.

Then the doors opened.

Sister Agnes entered, guided by an assistant. The room rose. David froze mid-sip. Linda's eyes widened.

The nun from the train.

David almost chuckled — the big donor, the African dignitary, the legend… had followed him off the subway, right into this room.

Linda, for her part, couldn't help but smile. She's the one? she thought. The soft-spoken woman with the old diary.

The meeting began. Introductions were made.

David's pitch was smoother than expected. Linda's policy alignment hit the right notes. Sister Agnes listened with calm focus.

But the truth was, the real meeting had already happened.

In the silence of a subway ride. In a shared walk through the city. In the quiet breakdown of assumptions.

That afternoon, a joint initiative was announced. Funding was secured. Headlines followed.

But none of them would ever forget the E train, seventh car, second seat from the right.

"Sometimes, the meeting isn't in the room.
It's in the ride that takes you there."

Chapter - 8
The Final Whistle

The Maracanã roared like a living beast.

Eighty-eight minutes had passed in the most important football match of his life, and young Lucas Almeida stood just outside the penalty box, his chest heaving, boots caked in turf and adrenaline.

A sudden stillness fell over him. Not on the field, but in his mind. The crowd disappeared, the commentators' shouts faded, and for a flickering moment, all he could hear was his father's voice.

"Show up on time, son. That's half the battle."

Lucas had heard it a thousand times. Growing up in Curitiba, his father was a school janitor who worked double shifts and still showed up for every weekend match, rain or shine. He believed in order, in discipline, in small, consistent acts.

Lucas, on the other hand, believed in flair. He skipped breakfast for futsal, was late to class, ignored curfews, and got benched more often than not for his attitude. He had talent — no one doubted that — but he burned through coaches like a cigarette. Fast, stubborn, unpredictable.

His father's words rolled off him like sweat: "Be polite." "Eat your greens." "Stretch after training." "Help your mother."

He rebelled with a sneer. He wanted to be like the stars on television — not some middle-aged janitor with calloused hands and outdated values.

Then came that night.

It was raining hard. They were driving home from yet another argument after Lucas stormed out of a match for being subbed off early. His father had tried to talk him down, but Lucas wouldn't stop.

He gripped the wheel too tightly. He drove too fast. He shouted something he would never repeat.

And then, out of nowhere, a deer. A horn. A crash.

The car spun.

He woke up in the hospital.

His father didn't.

The doctors said the seatbelt saved Lucas. The horn from the impact had pierced the windshield and hit his father directly in the chest. A one-in-a-million freak accident.

But, freak or not, it was the argument that haunted him. The words. The rage. The final moment he could never take back.

Lucas disappeared after that. Quit football. Refused to speak to anyone. He wandered through guilt and grief like a ghost until one day, he found his father's old duffel bag in the back of the closet.

Inside: a pair of whistle-worn cleats, a yellowed Santos FC scarf, and a notebook titled: "Lucas's Training Plan."

Every page was filled with dated entries: "Lucas skipped breakfast again. Make sure he drinks more water." "Coach says he's got raw talent. Needs polishing." "Lucas didn't stretch today. Tight hamstrings can break dreams." "Remind him: humility beats fame."

Lucas wept for the first time in months.

He showed up at the old field the next morning.

He ran. He trained. He ate the right food. He slept early. He made his bed. He said please and thank you. He was never late again.

Maracanã noticed.

His game sharpened. His stamina extended. His cards disappeared. He stopped trying to impress and started playing for the team. Coaches started calling again.

And today, he was here. On the biggest stage in Brazilian football. Because the team's regular striker — the star — had missed curfew after a party. The coach was furious.

Lucas had shown up. Early. As always.

"Discipline, not talent, gets you the starting spot," the coach had said.

In the 42nd minute, he remembered to thank the referee after a call went his way. The referee gave him a nod. Later, the same referee spared him a yellow card after a clumsy challenge — "You've got a good attitude, kid," the man had muttered.

His father's words again: "Kindness buys you more than talent ever will."

At halftime, the coach pulled him aside.

"You're light on your feet, son. What's your fuel?"

Lucas smiled. Boiled eggs. Cassava porridge. Water. Always water. His father used to wake up at five to pack him a balanced breakfast before games. He had resented it then. But in this game, while others wilted, Lucas sprinted.

He sprinted in the 60th minute. He slid in the 77th. He still had legs in the 88th.

And now — -the ball came bouncing out to him, just outside the box. The defenders were caught out of shape. He didn't think. He just moved.

One touch. Second touch. Left foot. Curl.

The net rippled.

The stadium exploded.

He collapsed to his knees, arms stretched to the sky, teammates piling on.

And then, as the roar of the crowd returned to his ears, he turned instinctively toward the stands.

And froze.

There, in the fourth row behind the dugout, stood his father.

Greying hair, Santos FC cap, hands cupped around his mouth in a cheer. Just like when Lucas was in college. Just like when they practised in the empty schoolyard at dusk.

For a moment, Lucas wasn't sure if it was real. His father had passed away two years ago — hadn't he?

He blinked. The man was gone. Or maybe never there.

But the glee on that face — that proud, familiar spark — remained. Seared in memory. Etched in victory.

Lucas raised the trophy that night not alone, but with every lesson, every lecture, every fatherly sigh packed into it.

Thc crowd saw a rising star.

Lucas saw his father's hand on his shoulder.

And for the first time since that rainy night, he didn't flinch. He smiled.

Because he knew, the final whistle wasn't the end.

It was the answer.

"Sometimes the loudest cheers are the ones that echo in your heart long after the whistle blows."

Chapter - 9

The Cave Beneath The White Wind

In the silent folds of the Eastern Himalayas, where the clouds skimmed the snowy ridges like wandering spirits, a blizzard crept in — quiet, white, and ruthless.

Three men — a disgraced monk, a desperate thief, and an ambitious village chieftain — would find themselves bound together in that storm.

Tenzin had once been among the most respected monks at the Tashi Rinpoche Monastery. Wise, calm, and deeply devoted. But not all monks wore their faith cleanly. Political infighting had spread through the temple like mildew on stone. Whispers became accusations. Accusations became exile. Tenzin was cast out for questioning the intentions of the new high lama — and most of all, for defending a sacred relic from being moved to please imperial guests.

The relic was the Golden Staff of Shenrab — an ancient artefact said to have belonged to the first spiritual teacher. It was a symbol of unity, not politics. But the new leadership had different plans. So did Chieftain Namgyal of the lower valley.

Namgyal was not cruel — but power had a scent, and he had caught its trail. His grip on the village was slipping, and a gift to the regional emperor might be just the lifeline he needed. Nothing spoke louder than relics.

And the Golden Staff, he believed, should not rot in a cold monastery. It should secure his name in the emperor's court.

Namgyal's plan was simple: retrieve the staff from the monastery's inner sanctum under the cover of darkness. But storms have no respect for schemes.

Caught in the blizzard, Namgyal was forced to seek shelter in a nearby cave.

There, he found two others.

The second man, thinner, younger, and bruised, was Norbu — a thief, once orphaned by the same monastery's rejection. Norbu had learned survival in back alleys, not mantras. That night, he had planned to rob the lower shrine for food and coin, but the storm swept him off his path.

And the third was Tenzin.

Three men. One cave. No names, not at first.

Tenzin lit a fire with flint from his robe. Namgyal offered dried meat. Norbu, shivering, stayed silent. Their breath curled in the frozen air.

"Fate enjoys irony," Tenzin said after a while.

"Or mockery," Namgyal replied. "I was supposed to be in the emperor's court tomorrow."

"Instead, you're in a cave with two strangers. Tell me, which court is wiser?"

They shared dry laughs. Later, Norbu broke his silence. "You're the monk who got thrown out, aren't you?" Tenzin raised an eyebrow. "And you are the boy who once tried to steal butter lamps from the winter altar."

Norbu smirked. "Didn't expect you to remember."

"I remember hungry eyes better than scriptures."

Namgyal listened. He hadn't realised who he was sitting beside.

Norbu muttered, "So, what now, monk? You're out. He's scheming. And I'm... just trying not to freeze."

Tenzin looked at the boy, truly looked. "You're not a thief. You're a reflection. Of what happens when temples forget compassion."

Silence again.

By morning, the storm had passed. The mountain glittered under the sunlight. They began descending — all three — toward the lower temple, where the Golden Staff was kept in a small sanctum.

That's when Tenzin understood. Namgyal's eyes lingered too long on the temple gates. His steps were too practised.

Inside, the moment came.

Namgyal tried to snatch the staff when the attendant bowed. The shrine trembled.

But Norbu stepped between.

"No," he said. Namgyal hesitated. "You? You're stopping me?"

"Not for the monastery," Norbu said. "Not even for the relic. For the monk who gave me tea in a blizzard. Who saw me? That's worth protecting."

Tenzin's voice followed, firm but calm. "Power taken is temporary. Power earned lasts lifetimes."

Namgyal lowered his hands.

That day, the staff remained.

Namgyal returned to his village — humbled, not disgraced. He never spoke of the cave.

Norbu stayed at the shrine, not as a monk, but as its quiet guardian.

And Tenzin? He was never invited back to the monastery. But he returned anyway — not for position, but for prayer.

The Golden Staff was never moved.

Because once, in a cave hidden by the white wind, three men changed their paths. Not with power, but with pause.

"Not every storm is meant to be endured alone. Some are sent to bring strangers together for what the world will never see — but forever feel."

Chapter - 10
The Cosmic Biscuit Incident

Eons ago — before humanity, before cities, and definitely before snack wrappers — three celestial beings from the star system of Vydanta arrived on a pristine little planet known as **Earth**.

They weren't on a mission. They were on vacation.

The galaxy had been loud, full of wars over solar spice and disputes about black hole zoning. Earth, however, was quiet. Lush. Peaceful. And most importantly, known for its **bananas**.

Onboard the sleek silver cruiser **Trimurti-7** were:

- **Brahma**: Biologist extraordinaire and cloning enthusiast, who packed more gene sequences in his belt than a typical planet could dream of.
- **Vishnu**: Diplomatic officer, navigator, and designated trip planner — the guy who never missed a sunset or forgot sunscreen.
- **Shiva**: Weapons chief and unofficial party starter, carrying twin laser cannons and a passion for spontaneous destruction (of the fun kind).

They descended gently into a green valley near the equator, parking their cruiser in a circle of wildflowers. Vishnu had even scheduled a picnic.

The moment they stepped out, things started going hilariously wrong.

Brahma's first step landed directly in an enormous pink lotus, which promptly latched around his leg like it had something to prove.

"Assist. Immediate assistance," he grumbled, flailing his upper arms.

"Again?" sighed Vishnu. Calm as ever, he activated his **navel extraction tether**, a long, coiling tool that emerged from his abdomen with a satisfying thwip. He gently yanked Brahma out with a pop and a squelch.

"Next time," said Vishnu, "check the ground for clingy flora."

Meanwhile, Shiva had already disappeared into the jungle, yelling, "FIELD TEST!"

Moments later, they heard bursts of laser fire and a gleeful "BOOM!" as a small hill was vaporised, a tree perfectly sculpted into the shape of a mango, and a pond lightly simmered.

He called it "terrain appreciation."

The trio laid out their galactic picnic, with Vishnu slicing bananas while Brahma inspected pollen samples.

In the distance, a group of **monkeys** cautiously observed.

"High curiosity," Brahma murmured. "Look at that one—trying to tie a vine into a swing."

"Leave them be," said Vishnu, chewing thoughtfully. "They're adorable, but let's not start anything."

But as they prepared to leave, something happened.

Brahma's pouch — the one with **experimental snacks** — slipped from his belt and fell near a patch of vines.

The trio didn't notice. The monkeys did.

Inside the pouch? A pack of **Strawberry Quantum Biscuits™.**

One bold monkey sniffed the wrapper, opened it with shocking dexterity, and devoured the first biscuit.

Generations later

The Trimurti returned to Earth for another vacation — but what they found was... baffling.

The trees were carved with images of **three beings with shining halos**. Fires danced in ritual circles. Statues stood tall in jungle clearings.

And among the creatures now walking upright and communicating with primitive yet poetic sounds, one word echoed repeatedly: **Manus**.

"Manus?" Vishnu asked.

Brahma froze. "Oh no."

"What?" Shiva said.

"That's... what I shouted when I realised my pouch was missing. It's a Vydantan word. Roughly means 'Oops squared.'"

The first monkey to eat the biscuit had apparently adopted the name as his title.

The Manus had become a legend.

The trio was stunned. Worshipped. Adored. There were tiny stone carvings of Shiva doing his laser dance. A temple with Vishnu's serene face carved in banana bark. A small mural of Brahma stuck in a lotus.

"Is that my forearms?" Brahma gasped.

"You look majestic," Vishnu smirked.

Shiva posed beside his statue. "Still got it."

And so, Earth — once a quiet escape — became their **favourite retreat**.

They brought family. **Indira**, Vishnu's cousin, adored the local cloud formations. **Ganesh**, Shiva's son, fell in love with the mangoes. Even Brahma warmed up to teaching the Manus poetry.

From galactic observers to accidental gods, they had become part of the planet's strange, beautiful story.

Thus, the evolution of Homo sapiens — the curious creatures we now call humans — began not with divine design, but with an experimental snack and a dropped pouch.

In every temple shadow, in every banana grove, in every curious pair of eyes, there echoes the legacy of a biscuit, a monkey, and three aliens who came for vacation… and never really left.

The End.

"Sometimes, the universe doesn't speak in big bangs or visions—just a snack rolling the wrong way, into the right hands, at the perfect time."

Chapter - 11
The Sandglass Protocol

Egypt, 2024. Under the hazy veil of a desert moon, two foreign researchers entered the Pyramid of Seti-Sutekh with flashlights that flickered too often, and motives they never voiced aloud.

Amelia Roth, MI6 operative with a doctorate in archaeology (for cover), had tracked ancient texts, whispered rumours, and stolen files to this precise location. The objective? A rumoured **temporal relic**, believed to have once manipulated time itself. She was methodical, sceptical, and slightly claustrophobic.

Jack Monroe, CIA field agent and part-time historian, had orders to secure the artefact at any cost. He had intercepted chatter in encrypted back channels: something powerful, hidden beneath Egyptian stone. He trusted no one. Not even his flashlight.

Both pretended to be strangers, meeting at the site entrance under a collaborative academic dig. But they knew.

They always knew.

Inside the pyramid, the air thickened. The walls oozed with heat and hieroglyphs. Every passage bent slightly wrong, as if space had a fever.

It was there, somewhere between the second and third corridor, that they met the boy.

He stepped from the shadows like a breath they hadn't taken yet.

"Tourists?" he asked, in perfect English.

Amelia stiffened. Jack instinctively reached for a non-existent holster.

"No," Amelia said. "Researchers."

The boy smiled. "Then you're going the wrong way. Unless you enjoy traps and sudden spikes."

He couldn't have been older than thirteen. His clothes were simple. His accent neutral. His eyes—ancient.

"What's your name?" Jack asked.

"Saif."

Saif didn't lead them as much as he shadowed them — observing, suggesting, occasionally warning. But it was Amelia's sharp analysis of wall carvings and Jack's uncanny instinct for architecture that uncovered hidden doorways and disarmed long-forgotten mechanisms.

"You two," Saif said at one point, with a grin, "are the best researchers I've worked with. Even I've never seen this deep inside."

Amelia gave him a look. "How many times have you been in here?"

He only smiled.

That necessity grew into something warmer. A near-miss triggered by a collapsing wall threw them into each other's arms — literally. After brushing off ancient cobwebs and shared laughter, Amelia squeezed Jack's hand just a little too long. Later, while crossing a creaking stone bridge over a pit of spikes, Jack steadied her waist and whispered, "Remind me to never take you on a first date to the beach."

"Why not?"

"No pyramids. No traps. Boring."

She smirked. "I like dangerous."

They moved deeper into the pyramid. The atmosphere grew heavier, stranger. Statues lined the corridor like guards. Whispers echoed without a source. Jack's watch spun backwards. Amelia's flashlight flickered blue.

Saif walked beside them, unusually calm. "You're close," he said. "To the prince's chamber."

"The prince?" Amelia asked.

Saif nodded. "The one who figured out time travel. He was famous in my day. Brilliant, feared, a bit dramatic. They say he could speak in thirty-two languages because he time-hopped through dynasties. Used to prank scribes by quoting poets who hadn't been born yet."

Jack raised an eyebrow. "Sounds like a legend."

"He was real," Saif said. "Clever. Wise. Handsome too, though he knew it. He always spoke like the universe owed him a biography."

Amelia smiled. "That's oddly specific."

Saif shrugged. "Maybe I just read a lot."

They reached the final chamber. A large **sarcophagus**, carved from dark granite marble, stood at the centre. Symbols glowed faintly under ultraviolet light. The air was fetid.

Jack stepped toward it. "We should open it."

Saif hesitated for the first time.

"I don't know if you should," he said. "It's... not really mine to protect."

"But you've come this far with us."

He looked away. "I'm just a guide in the shadows." Then added quietly, "Do what you feel is right."

Amelia and Jack stepped forward. Their hands brushed briefly over the stone — warm, familiar now. Together, they slid the lid open.

The room dropped ten degrees.

Inside, perfectly preserved, was **Saif**.

Mummified. Wrapped in ceremonial linens. A golden amulet on his chest.

Jack stumbled back. "What... what is this?"

Amelia whispered, "He's still here."

They turned.

The boy was gone. The torchlight flickered. No footsteps. No goodbye.

Just the faintest echo: "Unwise..."

Later, as they fled the pyramid, the memories unravelled strangely. Saif never touched anything. The pressure plates that should've triggered didn't seem to register his steps. He passed through tight spaces without rustling dust. Even in hindsight, they realized neither of them had ever actually touched him.

Was he a ghost? A loop in time? Or something that didn't need explanation?

Neither Amelia nor Jack ever spoke of that night. The artefact? They never found it. Or perhaps they did — and chose not to take it.

They returned home changed.

Two spies. One shared secret. One unsolvable mystery.

Over time, they would sit together — sometimes in silence, sometimes in laughter — and revisit the impossible question: Was it time travel? Space bending? Something supernatural? They never agreed. And perhaps, they thought, the truth was that it could be all three — layered like the pyramid itself, each answer buried within another.

Years later, they married. Not because of love at first sight. But because of what they'd shared in the dark — a boy who didn't belong, a chamber that bent time, and a choice not to understand it.

Some things... are better left mysterious.

The End.

"Sometimes the only way forward is to trust the guide."

Chapter - 12

The Forgotten Spark

The Caribbean sun shimmered across turquoise waves as **Alice** stepped barefoot onto the warm white sand, her family bustling behind her with cameras and beach bags. It was their first real vacation in years — a week of tropical bliss on a postcard-perfect island framed with jungle-green cliffs, banana-leaf breezes, and beachside smoothie stands that made even her father crack a rare grin.

Alice was only five, small for her age, with knees always scraped from adventures and fists full of found treasures. The island was a wonderland. She spent her days combing the beach, stuffing her pockets with shells, coral bits, and broken beads. She had always collected junk, ever since she could walk — a habit her grandmother adored.

“One day,” Grandma used to chuckle, “you’ll pick up something everyone else missed. You’ll find a real treasure, Alice. Mark my words.”

That day came when she spotted a **small, polished stone,** iridescent and strangely cold, half-buried near a cluster of driftwood.

It shimmered, faintly.

“Look at this!” she cried, stumbling toward her parents.

Her mother barely glanced. "Probably plastic, honey. Put it back."

Her older brother laughed. "You're going to build a museum of trash."

Only Alice felt the quiet hum of it in her palm. She washed it in the sea, whispered "mine" to herself, and tucked it into the side pocket of her backpack.

Back in Savannah, Georgia, the photos from that trip were printed and stuck to the fridge. The stone sat proudly on her little desk for a while — until colouring books and schoolwork began to crowd it out. Then it went into a drawer. Then the bottom of her wardrobe. Eventually, it ended up in a dusty box her dad labelled "Vacation 2012" and placed in the attic.

Time passed. So did childhood.

The sparkle in her eyes stayed, for a while, until the world got louder.

Then came COVID.

Her father's boat rental business closed during lockdown. Bills piled up. Her mother's hours were cut. They sold the car. Then the boat. They nearly sold the house.

Alice, now in high school, studied harder than ever. She wanted to become an astrophysicist; to chase stars the way she once chased shells. But university felt distant, like starlight that shimmered and never reached her.

She kept her head down. She stopped collecting stones.

At nineteen, Alice was quiet. Studious. Worn at the edges. Her family received notice that they had thirty days to vacate their rental. As they packed boxes, she volunteered to clean out the attic.

She found her old sketchbook first — stick figure astronauts riding meteors, a spaceship shaped like a dolphin.

Then a box.

Then the stone.

It shimmered.

Not with memory, but with light. Actual, real, breathing light. Faint at first, then pulsing with soft gold and deep cobalt, like an aurora inside a pebble.

Alice stared.

It hadn't done that in years.

She held it to the attic window. It sparkled differently at every angle. And suddenly, she remembered the beach. The wave sounds. Her grandmother's laughter.

And how no one believed her.

She had nearly stopped believing in herself.

That night, while her parents worried over rent, Alice searched online. She dove into forums, crystal ID chats, and archaeology threads.

And then she found it.

Viking Sunstones.

Ancient crystals. Used by sailors to find the sun, even when the skies were grey. Iceland spar. Rare. Powerful. A theory mentioned that one had gone missing during a westward expedition — perhaps ending up on a distant shore, pushed by centuries of tide.

The Caribbean.

Alice reached out — geology labs, curators, historians. She sent photos, then shipped the stone to a specialist.

Weeks passed.

The verdict: genuine Iceland spar. **Viking-era sunstone**.

Media attention followed. The story went viral. A collector made an anonymous offer.

The price was enough to clear her family's debts.

And fund her full ride to college.

Years later, Alice stood in a research observatory in Arizona, studying the spectra of exoplanet atmospheres.

Next to her keyboard sat a resin replica of the stone.

It didn't glow anymore.

But she remembered the attic. The dust. The weight in her hand. And her grandmother's voice:

"One day, you'll find a real treasure."

Serendipity, Alice realised, is rarely loud.

Sometimes, it's just a glimmer in a dusty box — waiting for you to believe in magic again.

The End.

"Sometimes what the universe buries, time returns—
when you're finally ready to see it."

Chapter - 13

The Girl Who Forgot to Die

Lausanne, Switzerland. Spring.

The cherry blossoms along Lake Geneva looked like pink whipped cream, and **Amélie Rousseau**, age nineteen, danced her way through them like the town's unofficial ambassador of optimism. Her days were a carousel of classes at EPFL, steaming cups of chocolate chaud from the train station kiosk, and long walks through cobbled lanes where tourists flocked to buy cowbells, handmade watches, tulip bulbs, and bars of overpriced nougat.

Amélie was a neuroscience student by day, prom queen by fluke, and full-time dreamer of parallel worlds. She lived life like it owed her sparkle.

Every weekend, she and her friends hiked the lavender-lined trails or took trains to alpine resorts. On one such trip to **Interlaken,** nestled between the sparkling lakes of Thun and Brienz and overlooked by the mighty Jungfrau, Amélie signed up for a paragliding adventure.

The sky was blue, the mountains crisp, and the air smelled faintly of melted chocolate and pine. They'd eaten fondue for lunch and taken dozens of pictures with sun-dappled goats. Amélie, in her favourite yellow jumper, felt untouchable.

As her harness clicked and the parachute spread like a petal, she shouted, “C’est magnifique!” ("It's magnificent!") she shouted before launching.

But high above the cliffs, something went wrong. A gust twisted the fabric. The glider dipped hard. Her instructor’s voice turned sharp. Straps snapped.

Below her, Interlaken twinkled in postcard stillness.

She fell.

In the minutes that followed, she could hear — shouts, ambulance sirens, distant sobs. She tasted blood. Lavender. She felt someone squeezing her hand. She tried to smile.

“Pas mal,” ("Not bad," she thought) she thought, woozy. “I saw Paris. I danced at the prom. I loved once. Good enough.”

And then, darkness.

Amélie woke up.

Which was unexpected.

The bed beneath her wasn’t her bed. The ceiling had seams and soft pulsing light. Her clothes were... not hers. White tunic. Soft boots. No tags. Her limbs moved with an uncanny lightness, like her body had been redesigned with new instructions.

Then came the people, kind-eyed, oddly dressed, speaking perfect French with the gentle rhythm of a different age.

"Où suis-je? ("Where am I?") she asked.

"Bienvenue au Centre de Re-Cognition, unité 14. Vous êtes en sécurité. ("Welcome to the Re-Cognition Center, unit 14. You are safe.")

Isekai? Was this real? Had she been reborn in a magical world?

Meanwhile, 500 years later — or technically, now — in a gleaming orbital campus above Mars, **Dr. Milo Vex,** a doctoral student at Neo-EPFL, was rummaging through long-forgotten data archives.

"Project: Human Brain" — a massive initiative launched centuries ago to map and preserve human cognition. The project had stalled, shelved due to technical limits and funding cuts.

But one sample had survived. Cryo-preserved. Perfectly.

A teenage girl named Amélie Rousseau.

She had donated her brain as part of an early collaboration between EPFL and **CERN**, on a very specific day in 2024—the same day a freak particle anomaly was registered at the Large Hadron Collider, creating a quantum signature never seen before.

That particle's burst was later identified as the key to quantum-level brain state preservation—the breakthrough that eventually made neural reanimation possible.

Unaware of all this, Milo, desperate for a doctoral project, pulled Amélie's brain from digital archives. What started as a theoretical personality simulation…

...became sentience.

Amélie was not a ghost or AI.

She had been reconstructed exactly as she was — her DNA restored, her memories intact, her consciousness stabilised through quantum latticework. In this future, brain cryogenics was as common as health insurance. Humans, routinely travelling for decades across star systems, now live 200–300 years.

But Amélie was unique.

She remembered everything. Her mother’s laughter. The aroma of fondue. Her cat Matisse. The green tram in Lausanne. And the terrifying beauty of Interlaken right before the fall.

Now, she was a sensation.

“The girl who forgot to die.”

Journalists interviewed her. Historians asked for stories. Children watched her stream, “Back Then,” where she explained school lunch queues, snowball fights, and what it meant to grow up without brain implants.

"You mean you had to charge your phones?" someone asked.

"Oui. And if you lost the charger, you begged everyone you knew."

Milo visited often. First out of academic duty, then genuine curiosity, and soon enough, friendship.

"You brought me back?" she asked one day.

He nodded. "Technically, I wrote the code. But you… woke yourself."

She smiled. "It's very on-brand. I once restarted my phone just by glaring at it."

She once asked Bloop, Milo's pun-loving bot assistant:

"So... I'm still me?"

Bloop blinked, then chirped: "You're you-er than ever. Quantum-certified."

She laughed so hard, Milo had to mute the med bay.

In time, Amélie found purpose again. She toured schools. Advised historians. Helped design the first holographic memory garden.

But most nights, she just sat by the observatory window, sipping replicated hot cocoa, watching Mars spin beneath her feet.

"Merci, CERN. Merci, Interlaken. Merci, broken parachute," ("Thank you, CERN. Thank you, Interlaken. Thank you, broken parachute,") she whispered once.

Because sometimes, the world doesn't give you a second chance.

Sometimes... it gives you five centuries.

The End.

Chapter - 14

The Brahma Kamal Moment

During the height of the COVID-19 pandemic, Raghav, a senior IT architect, made the life-altering decision to move back to India from Stuttgart with his wife Shubha and their two young daughters. The quiet hills of Uttarakhand seemed like the right place — a return to roots, to fresh air and the embrace of extended family. They moved into a modest ancestral home nestled near the foothills, where the fog clung to pine trees like secrets and the air still held the echoes of temple bells.

Living with them at the time was Raghav's elderly mother, a woman of unwavering faith and ritual. Every evening, she'd sit beside the tulsi plant and tell the girls stories steeped in Hindu mythology — tales of gods descending upon earth, of sages meditating for millennia, and of celestial blooms that appeared only in the presence of divinity. Among these, the story of the Brahma Kamal stood apart — a rare and sacred flower believed to bloom just once a year, always at night, and only in places touched by Lord Vishnu's blessings.

"Only the pure-hearted see it," she'd whisper. "And if it blooms in your home, know that God has walked through your door."

Botanists called it Saussurea obvallata, but to Raghav, that cold Latin taxonomy didn't begin to capture the flower's grace. The Brahma Kamal wasn't just a flower—it was a sign, a prophecy, a miracle in velvet white. When it bloomed, its petals unfurled like soft silk, exuding a subtle, otherworldly fragrance — a blend of jasmine, sandalwood, and the cool scent of Himalayan winds. It was said that the flower brought spiritual awakening and divine presence.

Raghav's mother had once told him the legend from the Mahabharata — when Draupadi, weary and longing, asked Bhima to find the mystical Brahma Kamal. Bhima, in turn, sought it from the far reaches of the Himalayas, encountering none other than Lord Hanuman himself, his brother. The flower became a symbol of impossible devotion and celestial grace.

A decade ago, on a spiritual trek to Kedarnath, Raghav had brought back a tiny sapling from a local sadhu who had blessed it with turmeric and ash. That first plant held all his youthful hopes — he even joked to Shubha that they'd name their second child after the flower if it ever bloomed. But fate had other plans.

The first plant was lost *during the chaotic move back to India. Amid packed boxes and farewell tears, it was forgotten on a German balcony in the heart of winter.*

The second, carefully potted and placed near their new Uttarakhand porch, was flattened in a freak monsoon landslide. Raghav was too consumed then — managing a late-stage Salesforce rollout for a global client, logging 16-hour days and chasing elusive milestones.

The third attempt? It wilted silently in the corner of his study, during a week-long deployment sprint when Raghav barely remembered to water himself, let alone the delicate plant. He noticed its drooping leaves only after it had already gone brown.

And now, the fourth plant. Taller. Healthier. Nursed in the mild sun, spoken to by Shubha every morning, occasionally visited by bees who seemed to hover just a second longer. But still... no bloom.

Ten years. Four attempts. No flowers.

Not yet.

That year, Raghav finally agreed to something his daughters had been begging for — a proper vacation. They chose Australia, drawn by the sun-drenched beaches, coral reefs, and the promise of doing absolutely nothing for two weeks. For once, Raghav left his laptop behind, tucked away his work phone, and let Shubha plan everything.

They surfed along Bondi Beach, wandered through the buzzing markets of Sydney, and tried their hands (rather clumsily) at making boomerangs in a local workshop. They strolled the lush vineyards of Yarra Valley, sipping sparkling grape juice while the girls rolled down grassy slopes. There were late-night gelatos in Melbourne, impromptu cricket matches with strangers, and a breathtaking hot air balloon ride over the Gold Coast.

For the first time in years, Raghav was not a man racing time. He was simply... present.

On their last evening in Australia, as they watched the sun dip into the Pacific from a clifftop restaurant, his younger daughter leaned on him and whispered, “This is my best day ever.”

He smiled. Maybe it was his, too.

When they returned to Uttarakhand, jetlagged and sun-kissed, the first thing the girls did was race to the back courtyard. Moments later, their shriek echoed through the house.

“Papa! The Brahma Kamal bloomed!”

Raghav rushed out. And there it was — a single, delicate bloom hanging from the most precious of his Saussurea obvallata vines. It had opened and wilted in their absence, its silky white petals now drooping like a curtain that had just closed after the final act.

For a moment, there was silence. Then came the quiet sadness.

“We missed it,” Shubha said softly.

But Raghav stood still, staring at the wilted flower, and then slowly began to smile. Not the forced smile of a man balancing deadlines and rituals, but something deeper. Warmer.

He realised something profound — that he had never been chasing the bloom at all. The flower had always been a symbol, not a goal. It's rare and silent bloom during their absence wasn’t a loss; it was a revelation. In that quiet, godless moment, the flower had whispered something sacred:

God is not in the rituals. He is in the laughter echoing in an empty courtyard, in the soft hum of a mother tying braids, in the sticky fingers from melted ice cream, and in the joy of being fully, wholly together.

Raghav understood now that divinity visits not through mantras or incense, but when a home is filled with love and presence. That week in Australia had been his Brahma Kamal moment — unassuming, fleeting, but powerful.

He turned to his daughters, hugged them tight, and whispered, "Next *year, we'll be watching together."*

The End

"Sometimes, while chasing rare flowers, we often miss the ones blooming right beside us."

Chapter - 15

The Bottle, The Map, And The Time That Waited

In the turquoise embrace of Vietnam's Ha Long Bay, where limestone karsts pierced the sky and the water glimmered with jade secrets, lived an old fisherman named Binh. A stoic man with a spine like driftwood and hands that told tales of decades spent untangling nets and weathering tempests. He lived in a stilted hut by the water with his wife Shien, their son Hung, and Hung's little daughter Linh.

Binh was not a man of letters. He spoke only Vietnamese and understood the rhythms of tides more than those of alphabets. One dusky evening, while rowing back from a particularly uneventful fishing trip, Binh noticed something bobbing in the tide. It was a bottle, old and worn, its greenish hue dulled by years of ocean wandering. Inside was a curled piece of parchment, browned with age and sealed with wax.

He brought it home, curious. Hung tried to peer inside but couldn’t get the wax unstuck. It lay on their humble kitchen shelf for months until Shien, Binh’s wife, tucked it away in her wardrobe beside an old jar of pickled mangoes.

Years passed. The bottle was forgotten.

Binh's life had been one of endless struggle — rising before dawn to battle the seas, sacrificing comfort to ensure that his only son Hung could study, learn, and dream. He sold the boat to buy Hung's textbooks. He fished through typhoons to pay for school uniforms. He ate leftover catch while Hung dined on dreams. And Hung did not disappoint. Over the years, Hung built a modest but rapidly growing seafood export business. With sweat, strategy, and relentless perseverance, he turned their family into one of the most respected merchant names in the region.

And that success paved the way for Linh, Hung's only daughter, to live a life far from struggle. She was carefree, confident, and charismatic — the very embodiment of a third-generation dream. By the time she was 21, she was already a Harvard student, breezing through classes in archaeology and maritime history, sipping matcha in Boston cafes, and snapping selfies by the Charles River.

She had grown up hearing tales of her grandfather's fishing days, often dismissing them as romanticised nostalgia. She didn't know of the blistered hands or missed meals — only that there were once nets and storms, and now there were housekeepers and annual Europe trips. "Ông nội was basically Moana," she'd joke with her college friends.

One summer, Linh returned to Vietnam for a cousin's wedding. Amidst laughter, lanterns, and the smell of lotus tea, Shien — now a silver-haired matriarch — was cleaning out old clothes from her wardrobe when the bottle tumbled out and cracked open against the tiled floor.

Linh picked it up.

The parchment, miraculously preserved, bore a spidery scrawl in French and English. She sat cross-legged that night with a lamp and her translation apps. Her perfectly manicured fingers trembled as she realised what she held.

It was a map. A detailed sketch of coordinates and an island outline marked with a red 'X'. The letter was from a panicked French pirate ship cook, a man named Jean-Marie Tussard, dated 1791.

"To whom it may concern," it began, "The ship 'L'Étoile du Sud' is sinking. Captain de Vienne is dead. We carry treasure looted from Indo-China, meant for the Emperor's vaults in Marseille. They forced me to cook, beat me when I spoke of escape. I cannot read the fancy map they keep. I drew what I could remember and sealed it in this bottle. God help you if you find this. They say gold lasts longer than kings."

Jean-Marie wasn't even supposed to be on the ship. A former pastry chef in Paris, he had been taken against his will and forced into service. He didn't understand navigation or treasure — he simply memorised what he could, drew it in panic, and hurled the bottle overboard just before the ship was torn apart by monsoon waves.

Linh was stunned. Her thesis advisor back at Harvard had once mentioned the legend of L'Étoile du Sud — a treasure ship rumoured to have sunk near Vietnam, never recovered. But this was no legend. This was the map.

The next months were a blur. Linh, with her university's backing, led an academic expedition. Hung, now a successful businessman but still the son of a fisherman, stood proudly on the dock as his daughter boarded the ship that carried her destiny.

It took weeks of sonar scans and oceanography, but eventually, they found it: a mangled wooden skeleton wrapped in coral and time, sitting quietly beneath a canopy of blue. Among the debris were coins, figurines, and ornate chests still sealed.

The media went wild. Museums clamoured. Experts debated.

But Linh didn’t take any for herself.

"We don’t need it," she said simply, echoing a humility she hadn’t known she had.

By now, her family had risen out of poverty long ago. Hung’s export empire thrived, and Linh’s life had been one of privilege. They had no hunger that gold could solve.

They donated the treasure to a maritime museum in Hanoi. Linh gave talks around the world on the discovery, but always credited a French cook who couldn't read maps, a bottle that chose its tide, and a grandfather who couldn’t read English.

Her closing line at one global conference in Geneva would be remembered long after:

"The universe isn't random — it's just patient. This treasure waited for centuries, skipping generations until it reached the one that didn't need it, only to remind us that time reveals value when we're ready to see it."

And so, from pirate hands to fisherman's net, through attic dust and American classrooms, the treasure of L'Étoile du Sud found its home again — not in gold, but in story, in legacy, and in the timeless, patient hands of serendipity.

The End

"Sometimes the past always finds its way home, even if it has to cross oceans."

Chapter - 16
The Island of Tomorrow

It began like any other long-haul flight—cramped seats, hopeful eyes, the smell of re-circulated air and microwaved meals. Flight AZ147, a twin-deck commercial behemoth en route from Sydney to San Francisco, carried 232 passengers, each carrying their own bundle of dreams, fears, and itineraries. No one suspected they were boarding a flight that would never reach its destination—nor that they would become part of a miracle hidden in plain sight.

There was the Japanese honeymoon couple in 14A and 14B, soft-spoken and radiant, snapping selfies, their fingers entwined like vines. In Row 28, a Kenyan tech entrepreneur named Jomo rehearsed his pitch deck for the Global Founders Summit. Nearby, in Row 5D, Meredith, a sixty-two-year-old Australian grandmother, clutched a letter she'd never dared to send to her son, now living in California. This was her first time crossing the Pacific.

In Economy Plus, a single dad, Marcus, juggled his squirming twins while dreaming of their first trip to Disneyland. A teenage girl, Zoe, sat beside them, headphones on, lost in her sketchbook. In First Class, Harold Chen, a sleepless executive, reviewed numbers that no longer mattered.

The captain, Callum Rourke, had flown for over 25 years. He had landed in typhoons, faced a mid-air engine fire once, and even successfully performed an emergency landing in a desert. He wasn't nervous when the first flicker hit. But when every screen turned black, including his dashboard, and the radio gave only static, he knew this was something else.

Over the next 12 minutes, the flight fell from modernity into madness. A high-altitude EMP drone had detonated—part of a series of attacks launched silently across continents. While the world's military powers postured and retaliated, passengers on AZ147 were staring at the seatbelt sign.

Callum, with no radio, no instruments, and no satellite GPS, descended through sheer instinct. Below, an uncharted coral-fringed island glimmered in the Pacific blue. It had no name. No history. It was as if Earth herself had saved one forgotten pearl for this very moment.

The landing was rough. There was screaming, water slapping, metal groaning—but the fuselage held. Every passenger survived. Even the luggage compartment stayed mostly intact.

Day 1 - The Landing

They couldn't believe it at first. The collective trauma had numbed them. But when they crawled onto white sands and realised no rescue was coming, denial began to crumble.

Phones were dead. Satellite signals were silent. Nobody came.

They set up makeshift camps with airline blankets and emergency kits. Captain Callum took charge with his crew. The passengers, dazed and scattered, began sorting themselves into something resembling order.

Jomo, the entrepreneur, teamed up with Zoe to organise water collection. Meredith, the grandmother, started a children's corner. Marcus built a cooking pit with help from an ex-Navy chef, now a retiree returning from visiting grandchildren.

The island had coconuts, edible roots, and a surprising number of freshwater streams. It was liveable. But the bigger question was—*why hadn't anyone come?*

Week 1 - The Questions

As the first few days passed, anxiety began to set in. Around the communal fires, whispers of *"Why us?"* and *"Why now?"* echoed between bites of roasted coconut. Meredith prayed every evening. Marcus stared out at the horizon as if willing a rescue helicopter into existence. Some thought they were cursed. Others wondered if it was divine punishment. The honeymooners cried quietly into each other's shoulders.

Harold Chen, the First-Class executive, finally remembered something vital—a satellite phone tucked into his business carry-on. Its battery was down to one bar, but it was enough.

He climbed with Captain Callum to the island's highest ridge and turned it on. Static. Then a signal. Then a burst of headlines from a world in chaos:

"Coordinated Drone Strikes Leave 12 Global Cities in Blackout." "Leaders Convene Emergency Summit in Geneva." "Limited Nuclear Exchange Reported in Northern Hemisphere."

They froze.

Not Armageddon. But something close.

Month 1 - The Perspective Shift

As the passengers absorbed the news, something changed. The despair turned into a strange sense of wonder.

"We were so busy cursing our fate," Meredith said one night, "but what if this was fate protecting us?"

Indeed, the war had damaged key cities, crippled digital infrastructure, and caused widespread confusion. But it wasn't total annihilation. Humanity survived. And so did they—unscathed by radiation, untouched by fallout.

Callum's emergency landing hadn't just saved them. It had bought them time. Time to live, reflect, and start anew.

They began to see the island not as a prison, but a sanctuary.

Year 1 - Rescue and Realization

Nearly a year after their disappearance, a solar-powered reconnaissance aircraft spotted smoke plumes over the island. Within a week, a hybrid naval vessel from the newly formed Pacific Federation arrived at their shore.

Tears, cheers, laughter. But also, reflection.

The world they returned to was changed—leaner, slower, wounded but wiser. Many of their homelands were still recovering, infrastructure rebuilding, governments re-forming.

And yet, the passengers of Flight AZ147 had something most didn't: peace. Unity. A bond forged by nature and sealed by survival.

Before they departed, Marcus carved words on a driftwood plank near the fuselage:

"We came here broken. We leave whole.
Chosen not by accident, but by grace."

Epilogue - The Legacy of AZ147

In the years that followed, books were written. Documentaries filmed. The survivors met annually to celebrate their "new birthdays." Zoe became an artist whose murals of the island were displayed globally. Meredith taught again, her island journals used as curriculum in post-crisis education systems.

And the island? Declared a global sanctuary—*Isola di Speranza*, the Island of Hope.

They never saw it coming. But they would never forget.

Because sometimes, what looks like a fall… is a flight.

Chapter - 17
The Knight of Ashwood Tavern

In the heart of downtown San Francisco, nestled between a neon-lit taqueria and a high-rise office complex, stood an old, rundown tavern with a crooked sign that read: "Ashwood Tavern." Once a local legend, the tavern had fallen into disrepair and bankruptcy after the mysterious disappearance of one of its owners' sons a few years ago. The story still clung like ivy to the memory of old-timers, whispered across barstools and in laundromats, carrying with it a certain eerie charm that made the building untouchable.

That is, until the Rivera family came along.

Hailing from Oaxaca, Mexico, the Riveras had moved to the U.S. in search of new beginnings. Martín Rivera, the father, had worked two jobs for over a decade before finally saving enough to invest in a property. When the Ashwood Tavern listing came up for auction, he saw potential where others saw only ghosts.

“We’ll make it into a café… maybe a panadería,” he told his wife, Lourdes, a brilliant baker known for her pan dulce and mole tamales. Their teenage son, Diego, wasn’t thrilled. At fifteen, he’d have preferred to stay in East Bay with his soccer buddies and less creepy buildings.

Still, he helped clean. Kind of.

One rainy afternoon, while sweeping out what used to be the storage attic, Diego found something beneath a dusty tarp: an old video game console with a tangle of wires and two clunky controllers. The label on the cartridge read, "The Princess of Eldoria."

Curious, Diego hooked it up to the dusty TV in the back room. Static crackled. The game whirred to life, showing pixelated knights, castles, and a princess trapped in a high tower by a dragon. It had a cheesy synth soundtrack and clunky dialogue. But the moment he selected “New Game,” everything changed.

A blinding white light surged from the screen, and in an instant, Diego was no longer in San Francisco. He awoke beneath a mossy oak tree in full armour.

The air smelled of lavender and pine. Towering mountains loomed in the distance. The sky shimmered with two suns.

“Whoa... ¿Dónde estoy?”

He looked around. A talking squirrel in a doublet informed him he had arrived in Eldoria. Diego was quickly dubbed “Sir Diego of the Fallen Star” by the local villagers after he defeated a band of goblins trying to loot the village grain reserves.

He took to the new world surprisingly well. Having grown up playing games like *Zelda* and *Elden Ring*, he was thrilled. Swords? Cool. Dragons? Awesome. Magic scrolls? Sign him up.

He studied Elvish spells under the watchful eye of Lady Amrynn, the forest sorceress, and learned swordsmanship from old Sir Balthor, a retired knight with a wooden leg and a weakness for potato stew.

But then came the darker tidings.

A once-famous knight, Sir Caelum, had turned to dark magic and become the Demon Lord, ruling the obsidian mountains of the east. Many believed he was once the hero of Eldoria who, after saving the princess, chose to stay and conquer rather than return.

"Power blinds," Lady Amrynn warned. "Even the noblest hearts can lose their way."

Diego trained harder. He joined forces with dwarves, befriended a grumpy griffin, and even helped save a gnome town from a gelatinous cube invasion. His legend grew, and eventually, he faced the Demon Lord in a battle of fire and fury.

Steel clashed. Spells lit the sky. The castle trembled as Diego drove his sword through the Demon Lord's heart.

The dark helm rolled off.

Underneath was a young man with kind eyes and a resigned smile.

"Gracias… for reminding me who I was," he whispered.

Light returned. Diego was once again in the attic, the old console sparking one final time before going dark.

Had he dreamed it all?

He rushed to tell his parents, but they were busy making tamales for their new café's soft launch. Diego kept it to himself. Maybe he just needed sleep.

The next day, the café opened. The neighbourhood came alive with smells of pan dulce and laughter. A man entered—tall, quiet, with a scar on his jawline and a gentle presence. He ordered a café de olla and, before leaving, leaned close to Diego and whispered:

"Gracias por salvarme. I changed the game's ending because I couldn't let go. Saving the princess… it changed me. But greed did the rest."

Diego's eyes widened.

The man winked. "Don't worry. This time, I'm staying logged out."

And just like that, he was gone.

As Diego looked around at the once-haunted tavern now filled with warmth, food, and laughter, he realised some magic was real — and some games weren't just meant to be played. They were meant to be lived.

The End

"Sometimes the games in the universe worth playing are the ones where you don't return the same"

Chapter - 18

Bag 007 And the Summer Of Shifts

When the summer break began, neither Aanya nor Élise imagined they would be spending it with someone else's wardrobe—and worldview.

Both were international students at a U.S. university. Aanya hailed from Pune, India—sharp-tongued, observant, and always draped in the flowy comfort of a salwar kameez. Élise was from Lyon, France—fashion-forward, confident, and firmly loyal to crop tops, linen shorts, and minimalist black.

They shared a few classes but shared nothing else. Not views, not friends, and certainly not respect for each other's fashion sense. Aanya found Élise's clothes too revealing and impractical. Élise thought Aanya dressed like someone's grandma.

And then came the mix-up at JFK Airport.

Both had the same matte navy-blue Samsonite, the same model, bought during the university's Black Friday luggage fair. Both had left the combination lock at the default: 007. Bond would've sighed.

Aanya was headed to Tanzania for a public health research internship. Élise was flying to Mongolia to join a conservation project studying the migration of wild horses. Neither realised the mistake until they reached their respective destinations, opened the suitcase, and stared in confused horror.

"Crop tops? Where are my long cotton kurtas?"

"Salwar kameez? And what is this—homeopathic pills in a tin box?"

They emailed each other instantly through the university's portal. Mild panic turned to awkward apologies. Then came an odd détente.

Élise: "You know, these fabrics are actually... breezy."

Aanya: "I never thought I'd wear ripped jeans. But I feel kinda badass."

With a laugh and a virtual pinky swear, they decided to spend the summer using each other's wardrobes—with mutual permission. "Let's walk in each other's shoes," Élise had typed. "Literally," Aanya replied.

In Tanzania, Aanya found herself slowly shedding layers—not just of clothing, but of self-doubt. Her internship involved fieldwork under scorching sun, long hikes, late-night data crunching, and team bonding with people from 12 countries. She wore Élise's loose tanks and athletic shorts, first reluctantly, then with surprising ease. Nobody judged her.

What surprised her most was the confidence she found—not in the clothes, but in herself. She stood straighter. She laughed louder. She even danced once, barefoot by the fire, under the stars.

In Mongolia, Élise discovered function over fashion. The salwar kameez, with its breathable cotton and loose fit, proved perfect for long treks and cultural meet-ups with nomadic families. She even learned to tie a dupatta in six different ways, including as a headscarf during a sandstorm.

But what truly changed her was the reaction of the women she met—older Mongolian ladies who touched the fabric reverently and asked where it was from. She explained, with growing pride, that it was Indian.

As weeks passed, Aanya and Élise began exchanging voice notes.

Aanya: "I wore your red tank today to a village school. The kids loved the stickers I brought. I felt like a rockstar teacher."

Élise: "Your green kurta saved my life today. Horse kicked up a storm of dust, but I wrapped the dupatta around like a ninja."

They started following each other on Instagram. Aanya posted a sunset selfie wearing Élise's shades. Élise uploaded a slow-motion twirl in Aanya's mustard kurti.

By the time summer ended, the suitcases were secondary. What mattered was the journey of becoming—one patterned scarf, one unexpected compliment, one strange recipe at a time.

Back in their dorm hallway, the long-awaited reunion came with zero fanfare. They met, smiled, and hugged like old friends. No apologies. No awkwardness.

“Next time,” Élise smirked, “let’s just swap closets on purpose.”

“Deal,” said Aanya. “But I’m keeping the sandals. They’re magic.”

That summer, neither girl returned the same. They had walked miles in each other’s clothes—and come home with each other’s strength.

And the luggage? Still the same. Still 007.

Just like the code to an unexpected friendship.

The End

“Sometimes, it takes wearing someone else’s clothes to feel comfortable in your own.”

Chapter - 19

The Jade, The Ghosts, And the Serendipity Of 666

Long before the noise of scooters and subway tunnels rattled through the Middle Kingdom, in a valley swept with silk breezes and cherry blossoms, there stood a palace unlike any other. Built of lacquered wood, gilded eaves, and moonstone tiles, the Wu An Palace was once the crown jewel of ancient Southern China. At its heart was a princess named Lianhua — a fiery, proud young woman who was more stubborn than the stone lions at the palace gates.

She was beautiful, yes, but also impossible. Lianhua had a temper sharper than any blade in the royal arsenal. She refused to apologise, ever — not to servants she scolded harshly, not to suitors she humiliated in debates, not even to her mother or the emperor himself. "I am right by birth," she would proclaim. Her arrogance was legendary. She believed an apology was a sign of weakness and humility, a servant's virtue, not hers. Her courtiers feared her. Her peers avoided her. Her father, the emperor, despaired. The entire empire tiptoed around the whims of Princess Lianhua.

When her father died in a tragic hunting accident, the lonely halls of Wu An grew quieter. Her arrogance gave her strength, but left her with no one to grieve with. On the night of the funeral, a Tibetan mystic brought her a gift — a jade statue, carved with the symbol of the lotus. "For serenity," he said. "But beware. A soul too proud to weep becomes the prisoner of its own echo."

She scoffed, of course. That same night, she was found lifeless in the courtyard, clinging to the jade. Her soul, imprisoned by that final moment of pride, became trapped inside. Her stubbornness had anchored her to the earth. She had never said sorry, and that omission sealed her fate.

Locals avoided the palace for centuries, whispering tales of eerie laughter, inexplicable drafts, and doors that creaked open without wind. One such tale tells of two robbers who tried to loot the palace in the year 732. As they tiptoed through the dust-laden corridors, the jade statue spoke. One robber screamed. The other fainted. Both died of heart attacks — and promptly joined the princess in her ghostly misadventures.

Over the next 3,000 years, the palace collected accidental ghosts like lint. Some died of fright. Others slipped on wet tiles. A few were just in the wrong place at the wrong haunting. Peasants, blacksmiths, tailors, soldiers, poets, monks, bureaucrats, herbalists, students, engineers, and even real estate agents. By the time the Ming dynasty passed, over 300 ghosts roamed its halls. By the early 2000s, there were 666.

Princess Lianhua, who once enjoyed her solitary haunt, now shared space with loud, bickering spirits. She tried to escape to the rafters, then the cellar shrine. Nowhere was quiet. Finally, exasperated, she locked herself back into the jade statue, retreating into spiritual slumber.

Part II: The Journey of Jade

In 1795, during a local warlord raid, the jade statue was taken from the ruins of Wu An Palace. It passed into the hands of a southern king who placed it in his court as a lucky charm. Later, during the Opium Wars, it was seized by British officers and taken aboard a ship en route to England. That ship? The *Titanic's* sister cargo vessel, the *Oberon*, narrowly escaped iceberg-infested waters by sheer coincidence.

From there, the jade bounced through auctions, diplomatic gifts, and inheritance squabbles. During the French civil unrest in 1848, it was hidden inside a breadbox and mistaken for a rolling pin. In World War I, it was stored in a British underground vault and nearly lost to a bomb strike. In World War II, a German officer tried to smuggle it out of Paris but was distracted by an accordion parade and abandoned the crate.

Eventually, the jade reached the British Museum in London under the vague title "Oriental Curio — Late Qing Dynasty." Locked behind glass, it sat quietly for decades, overlooked by historians who assumed it was just ornamental.

Lianhua saw it all. Though locked in her jade shell, she absorbed the world: the shifting languages, the progress of trains, electricity, aeroplanes, and finally smartphones. She heard laughter in cafes, arguments on radios, and lullabies sung to sleeping children. The world moved, softened, changed.

Part III: Return Of the Jade

In 2023, flamboyant Chinese real estate magnate Mr. Jin won the jade statue at an elite New York auction. He had recently acquired the ruined Wu An Palace grounds with plans to build a luxury seven-star resort — complete with spa, jade museum, and rooftop pagodas.

He had the jade flown back to China, installed in the palace's central hall, atop a golden pedestal etched with "666" — a feng shui consultant's idea to attract wealth and cosmic harmony.

The moment the jade touched the palace floor; a ripple echoed through the ghost realm.

She's back.

Spirits stirred. Ming Dynasty magistrates poked their heads from scroll rooms. Han warriors blinked awake. An 80s IBM technician straightened his tie. All of them gathered.

Princess Lianhua awoke — dazed, slightly annoyed, and confused. "Who brought me back?" she demanded.

"We missed you," said a ghost with half a broom.

"You were the core of this place," whispered a Tang-era scholar.

"You were insufferable," added the peasant girl from the well. "But we were worse."

"And... we never thanked you," muttered the monk.

She paused. Something heavy lifted from her soul. Her eyes shimmered. She had seen so much across time — joy, grief, growth. She had seen artists die poor, and their paintings were adored centuries later. She had seen orphans become scientists, empires fall and rise, and strangers hold hands on rainy evenings. And in that moment, surrounded by those who once annoyed her to no end, she saw the truth:

She had never chased the bloom. She was the bloom. But it took 3,000 years of stillness, motion, solitude, and serendipity to learn it.

Her voice trembled. "I'm sorry."

And the heavens cracked open with light.

One by one, the ghosts smiled and ascended — 666 tiny stars vanishing into the cosmos.

Epilogue: The Luck of 666

Mr. Jin's hotel opened in 2025 to international fanfare. People reported strange peace, inexplicable comfort, and the best night's sleep of their lives.

The jade statue, now housed beneath a glass dome with the lucky "666" emblem, drew countless visitors. None suspected the true power it once held.

They assumed the number was for wealth. It was.

But the wealth was not gold or fortune — it was peace, reconciliation, and the release of centuries of stubbornness… in the most serendipitous haunting of all time.

The End

"Sometimes all it takes is an apology to move the universe in your direction"

Chapter - 20
The Coconut Awakening

It was with a sudden jolt that I woke up.

And when I say *jolt*, I don't mean some metaphorical enlightenment or poetic sunrise moment. I mean *actual, literal jolt* — something whacked me right on the forehead. Not figuratively. *Thud.* Like a heavy thump delivered by nature's version of a bowling ball.

I opened my eyes to the most confusing scene: a group of people in dhotis and lungis running around, a crying woman holding a brass plate of camphor flames, and the distinct scent of burnt turmeric in the air.

I had no clue where I was. But the pain in my head was very real. And next to me? A broken coconut. Still rolling.

Flashback: One Week Earlier

According to local legend (and my extremely chatty uncle, who recounted this to every media outlet within 200 kilometres), I was in a coma.

Yes. A genuine, medically diagnosed, fully unresponsive coma.

No, I wasn't in a hospital in Switzerland, but in a government hospital in southern Tamil Nadu, near a temple town known less for miracles and more for spicy snacks.

Apparently, after a minor bike accident (caused by my attempt to chase a street dog that had stolen my vada), I ended up with a head injury and slipped into a coma.

Doctors tried everything.

IV drips. CT scans. Loud music. One nurse even tried playing *Enna Solla Pogirai* on loop next to my ears. Nothing worked.

Until fate — and gravity — intervened.

The Coconut Conspiracy

On the seventh day of my coma, my relatives decided to shift me to a nearby temple for "divine intervention." (Apparently, temple therapy scores just below MRI in some circles.)

So, there I was, unconscious and horizontal on a bamboo stretcher, being paraded near a 300-year-old coconut tree next to the temple gopuram.

And then — **the serendipitous thud**.

A coconut, ripe and ready, fell at *precisely* the moment the stretcher rolled underneath. It cracked my forehead like a divine reset button.

I bolted upright.

Gasps. Screams. Someone fainted (ironically, not me this time).

The priest dropped his bell. The temple elephant looked confused.

But I, dear reader, had awakened — not by medicine, not by prayer, but by a mid-air tropical fruit, courtesy of gravity and poor tree maintenance.

The Aftermath

Local news channels went berserk.

"Coconut Revives Coma Patient!"

"Is Lord Murugan Working Through Palms?"

"Fruit or Fate? The Miracle of Maranthai Village!"

One local YouTuber even launched a channel called *Coconut Chronicles*, dedicated to fruits causing divine interventions. (Episode 3 was just a mango falling on a scooter, but still.)

My family, of course, was overjoyed. They now considered that particular coconut tree a *living deity*. It got garlands, camphor, and even a protective grill — just to preserve future miracles.

But what no one noticed was how serendipitous this was.

The True Twist of Serendipity

You see, my coma wasn't just a nap. It was — let's say— crowded. I had dreams within dreams. Whole déjà vu sequences. I remember *everything*: a mysterious temple, flying cars, coconut-shaped spacecraft, colours that didn't exist in this dimension. There was even a squirrel in a dhoti who told me I had "unfinished karma."

But now that I was awake, it all vanished.

Except... I *knew* things. I started predicting people's sentences. I once walked into the hospital canteen and told the cook not to add salt, because the rice cooker had already overflowed. He dropped the ladle and stared at me like I was the coconut avatar of Nostradamus.

Was it divine? Was it science? Was it... a delayed side effect of hospital sanitiser?

Who knows?

All I know is, **I went into a coma chasing a vada, and came out with an unexplainable insight into life.** And it all happened because a coconut, of all things, had perfect timing.

Epilogue: The 5-Star Fruit

Today, that coconut shell is framed in our house like a national treasure.

Visitors are shown the sacred dent on my forehead — slightly crescent-shaped, very prestigious.

Every time someone asks, "What brought you back?"

I reply with a smile:

"Just a little head-butting with destiny. Powered by serendipity. And one very punctual coconut."

The End

"Sometimes miracles can come as accidents"

Chapter - 21
The Eye of The Storm

Twenty-nine-year-old Rukmini Devi had never stepped beyond the borders of her small Tamil Nadu village. Her world was one of paddy fields, modest clay homes, and monsoon calendars. Each day began with folded palms toward the rising sun and ended with calloused hands returning from the fields, her two-month-old daughter tied gently to her back with a cotton sari.

Her daughter was her world. Named Kaaveri, after the life-giving river, she was born on a particularly stormy night, under flickering oil lamps and panicked whispers. Villagers said the gods touched children born under such tempests. Rukmini simply held her baby tighter and prayed for calm winds.

But nature had other plans.

One October afternoon, as dark clouds gathered ominously above the rice paddies, Rukmini was knee-deep in muddy water. Kaaveri lay cooing in a straw crib under the shade of a neem tree nearby. The winds, gentle at first, suddenly howled with a fury Rukmini had never known. She turned just in time to see a colossal gust lift the crib off the ground.

"No!" she screamed, running toward the tree.

But it was too late. The storm, a monstrous cyclone of historic proportions, picked up the child like a fragile dandelion and swept her into the grey horizon.

Rukmini collapsed.

Villagers found her the next day, unconscious, clutching a strip of the baby's blanket. Kaaveri was declared lost. A miracle storm, the press called it. One of the worst in the decade. Over 400 lives lost. Among them, a baby girl, whose name only her mother remembered.

Meanwhile, 500 kilometres away

In Kanyakumari, on the balcony of an old seaside colonial bungalow, two Swedish climate scientists—Henrik and Freja Lindström—had been huddled under thick tarps, waiting for the storm's wrath to pass. They had come to India as part of a global research team studying monsoonal patterns and climate change in the Indian Ocean.

Freja, exhausted, clutched a warm mug of coffee. "We should evacuate next time," she muttered. "This is madness."

Henrik squinted through the pouring rain.

And then they heard it.

A soft, gurgling cry—eerily out of place amidst the howling wind. Freja turned and gasped. Tangled in seaweed and cloth, cradled miraculously on their balcony, was a baby. Alive. Wailing.

"This can't be real," Freja whispered.

But it was. As if the storm had reached into the chaos, plucked the child from death, and placed her at their feet.

They reported it, of course. The village was in ruins. Records destroyed. No one claimed her. After months of inquiries and paperwork, the baby was adopted. They named her Astrid, meaning divine strength.

25 Years Later: Geneva, Switzerland

The grand hall of the United Nations Headquarters buzzed with tension. A pivotal vote was hours away. At stake: a controversial proposal to clear 600,000 acres of tropical forest in Southeast Asia to construct a mega-dam designed to curb future cyclones.

The world was divided. Corporates and governments backed it. Climate activists opposed it. It was pitched as a necessary evil. The science, however, remained murky.

And one of the fiercest voices *for* the proposal was none other than Rukmini Devi, now 54, an eloquent, respected voice from the Global South. Years after her tragedy, Rukmini had emerged as a climate resilience expert, passionately advocating infrastructure development to prevent future storms like the one that had taken her daughter.

Rukmini stood with quiet dignity, her sari crisp, her glasses perched perfectly. She was unmoved by protests. She knew what it felt like to lose a child. Prevention mattered more than sentiment.

Across the aisle, a young woman paced nervously.

Astrid Lindström, 25, climate policy scholar, Harvard graduate, and representative of the Nordic Green Bloc, adjusted her notes. She had lobbied for two months, but votes were slipping away. Big construction companies had poured millions into counter-lobbying. Astrid's proposal to explore ecological alternatives had been drowned in noise.

Her final speech was her last chance.

When she stepped to the podium, the hall stilled.

"I am not here to change votes," she began. "I am here to tell a story."

She spoke of a storm. Of a balcony in Tamil Nadu. Of a baby who should've died. Of a miracle. She spoke of her Swedish parents who loved her, and the unanswered questions about her origins. She told the room how her existence was born from the very climate chaos this dam sought to solve.

"Nature is not vengeful," she said. "It is not kind either. Nature simply *is*. And for every story of loss, there is a story of life. We cannot act on fear alone. We must act on wisdom."

Silence.

Rukmini looked up.

Her heart thudded.

The resemblance.

The same deep black hair. The curve of the jaw. The eyes.

And then Astrid turned to her and smiled. It was the smile of a baby Rukmini had cradled decades ago.

Her hand trembled.

The vote was called.

To everyone's shock, Rukmini raised her hand *against* the proposal.

It passed. By one vote.

Epilogue

Later that day, in the corridor, Astrid approached her.

"I think… I think I'm your—"

Rukmini didn't wait. She pulled her into an embrace, tears streaming.

"You've always been mine."

It had taken 25 years, two storms, and a miracle on a balcony — but mother and daughter, once torn by winds, were now united by will.

Serendipity, they say, is not coincidence. It's grace in disguise.

The End

"Sometimes the threads broken can be woven once again by time"

Chapter - 22

The Goat That Stopped The War

It was a humid morning in the village of Bhairavpur, nestled somewhere between Nowhere and Absolutely Nowhere Else. Cows mooed in the background, a rooster was chasing a surprised postman, and old Ram Lal was fiddling with his trusty Nokia 1100. The goats were sick again. Something about the bowels, he thought. It was time to call Dr. Madan, the local veterinarian, who usually fixed everything from limping cows to lovesick buffaloes.

"Nine-eight-seven-three-double-five-eight-three," Ram Lal muttered, squinting at the scribbled note on the back of a fertiliser packet. His thumbs, like those of a man who had eaten too many samosas and held too many farming tools, punched the numbers.

Except that one digit was off.

Far away in Langley, Virginia, inside a secure office filled with monitors, blinking lights, and an intimidating number of acronyms, CIA Deputy Director Charles W. Pickering III's red emergency satellite phone rang.

He stared at it.

Nobody called that number.

He answered, cautiously: "This is Eagle Nest One. Identify."

Ram Lal, now yelling over a very loud goat, replied in crisp Bhojpuri:

"Madanjaee! Dekha na, e bakri ke pet kharab baa! Char din se gobar na aail ba! Ka kari?" (Madanji! Look, this goat has a stomach issue! It hasn't pooped in four days! What should I do?)

Pickering sat up straight. He didn't understand the language, but years in intelligence had taught him to recognise tone and urgency. Also, the phone number was one that only high-clearance field operatives used.

His assistant, Jody, whispered from across the room, "That sounded like a regional dialect from North India."

"Run a decryption," Pickering said. "This could be code. Repeat: This. Could. Be. Code."

Jody tapped into her AI-powered linguistics software. The translation popped up: *"The goat hasn't pooped in four days."*

"A goat," murmured Pickering. "Could be a metaphor. Code for a stalled operation? Or an asset compromised?"

Ram Lal continued: "Aur humra lagat ba ke o chara theek na ba. Bhor me chara khailas, tab se baaithal baa." (And I think it's the grass. She ate something weird in the morning and now she just sits there.)

"Asset immobilised after exposure. Possibly bad intel or corrupted data feed," Pickering said aloud, eyes narrowing.

The conversation continued. Ram Lal, getting increasingly annoyed that Madanji wasn't prescribing anything useful, began describing the goat's entire feeding history.

"Goru ke khurak kha le rahi. Ee bakri samajhat ba ki o goru baa.” (She ate the cow's fodder. She thinks she’s a cow!)

Jody nearly dropped her coffee. "Sir... if we interpret this loosely, it’s as if someone infiltrated the wrong unit, perhaps someone impersonating a higher-tier operative."

"A mole? Disguised as one of ours? Holy hell."

Pickering stood. "Get me STRATCOM. Tell them Operation Albatross is on indefinite hold. We’re scrubbing the operation and re-evaluating intel sources."

Within 40 minutes, Operation Albatross — a precision strike on a high-value enemy target — was aborted. Satellites were recalibrated. Diplomats were quietly told to stand down. Media blackouts were issued.

Meanwhile, Across the Border...

In a secure military outpost, General Anwar Reza of the Eastern Alliance was baffled.

"They didn’t strike. Why didn’t they strike? They *always* strike on Tuesdays. What do they know that we don’t?"

His deputy shrugged. "Sir... maybe they know we know. And now they know we know they know."

Anwar blinked. "This is too confusing. Call the ambassadors. It’s time to talk."

Back In Bhairavpur...

Ram Lal was still yelling into the phone. "Kahe chup ho gail baa? Ka ilaaj baa ke na? (Why did you go quiet? Is there a cure or not?)"

Pickering, lost in the chaos of global diplomacy, had forgotten to hang up.

Finally, Jody clicked the line closed. "Sir, you think we should trace the number?"

Pickering exhaled. "No. Whatever op that was, the agent was... unconventional, but effective."

Six Weeks Later...

Peace talks began. Intelligence suggested both sides were at the brink of irreversible damage. But the absence of a trigger had forced reflection.

Historians would later call it *The Quiet Tuesday* — the day war didn't begin.

No one knew the real reason.

Except Ram Lal, whose goat was finally feeling better after Dr. Madan arrived that evening with a packet of Ayurvedic goat laxatives.

And deep in the CIA, Pickering kept a photo on his desk of a very smug-looking goat, printed from the decryption software's notes.

Underneath the photo, a single phrase was written:

"Code Name: Serendipity."

The End

Chapter - 23
God Mode

Naveen and Felix were two overworked, under-showered students at MIT who spent more time on their favorite video game, *Dominion Era*, than they did on classes. The game was part empire-building, part village management, and part divine intervention. Think Age of Empires, but with way more praying villagers.

"Watch this," Naveen said, slouched in a bean bag, holding a controller sticky with pizza grease. "This little guy's been praying for two days straight. Look at his devotion bar! If it hits 85%, I get free mana."

Felix squinted at the screen. "Dude, you're bribing digital people with divine gifts. That's basically micro-managing faith."

"Exactly! That's how you win in *Dominion Era*. Make them believe. The more they pray, the more bonuses you get. Faith equals farming speed, mining boost, mood upgrade, you name it."

On the screen, inside the village of Lurovia, a digital monk named Brother Galen knelt at a pixelated temple.

"O Great Ones of Light and Wi-Fi," he muttered. "We humble ourselves for food, guidance, and better harvests."

Behind him, a carpenter named Mara raised an eyebrow. “You sure the gods are listening, or are you just hungry?”

Just then, a golden beam came from the sky. A crate of food landed beside the temple with a soft thud.

Mara blinked. “Did… did that just happen?”

Galen raised his hands. “Behold! A miracle from the heavens!”

Back in the dorm, Felix laughed. “Okay, that was me. I gave them food because that monk has a killer prayer streak. Ten in a row!”

Naveen leaned back. “Man, sometimes I feel like they believe in us. It’s weird. Like we’re actual gods to them.”

Felix sipped his energy drink. “Yeah, except we’re broke, sleep-deprived college kids eating instant noodles. Real divine.”

Meanwhile, inside the game world…

Brother Galen scribbled in his scroll: *“The gods favour effort. They are mysterious, powerful, and possibly smell like stale cheese.”*

Mara scoffed. “What if the gods are just… dudes? Like us?”

Galen smirked. “Then I hope they’re better at managing resources.”

Somewhere far, far away — in a different universe — a glowing orb floated in a giant, silent chamber. It showed Naveen and Felix on a screen.

An alien entity, shaped like a jellyfish with Wi-Fi signals for hair, watched them.

"They're playing a game," the jellyfish-being muttered.

Another alien floated by. "Isn't *their* world a simulation we built?"

"Exactly," said the jellyfish-being. "So now we're watching simulated creatures simulating other creatures who believe they're gods."

The second alien blinked. "That's… deep."

"No, that's hilarious."

Back at MIT…

Felix yawned. "You ever think we're in someone else's game?"

Naveen grinned. "Like some alien student is watching us goof off and thinking we're the villagers?"

Felix laughed. "Yeah, and they're like, 'Why aren't these guys farming?! They're just playing video games!'"

On screen, Brother Galen looked up at the sky. "The gods seem… distracted."

Mara pointed to a glitching chicken. "Maybe they're busy debugging."

The next day, a strange notification popped up in *Dominion Era*:

“Event Unlocked: Recursive Faith.”

Neither of the boys knew what that meant.

But deep in the jellyfish-being’s universe, a new file was created:

“Simulation Status: Observing Humans Playing Gods Who Think They’re Being Played by Gods.”

Under it, a note appeared:

“Subject 23: Serendipity triggered.”

Because sometimes, being a god is just a matter of perspective. And sometimes, the real joke is who’s watching whom.

And if you're wondering who made the jellyfish-being?

Well… that’s a story for another chapter.

The End

Chapter - 24
The Mahabharata Decryption

It began with a missed turn on a research expedition. A group of scientists from Geneva, deep into Himalayan terrain for climate fieldwork, found themselves lost amid the lush yet unforgiving forest trails of Uttarakhand. Clouds brewed overhead, GPS failed, and the satellite phone blinked its last bar. Just as panic began to simmer, they saw a plume of smoke winding up through the trees—an ancient ashram, untouched by time.

Led by Dr. Aryan Dev, a physicist known for his work in quantum field theory and deep AI modelling, the group approached the ashram hoping only for directions and some drinking water. What they found instead was a man sitting serenely by a crackling campfire, his saffron robes fluttering in the breeze. His face was ageless, neither old nor young, and his eyes carried the calm of someone who had seen many lifetimes.

"Welcome," he said, before they could speak. "I've been expecting you."

The scientists exchanged nervous glances. Had this man somehow received their coordinates? Was he part of a research base?

"I am Rishi Varenya," the man continued, "Custodian of memories long buried beneath myth."

The group sat. Something in the air, perhaps the clarity of the mountain wind or the sheer oddity of the moment, convinced them to listen.

That night, as the others dozed off, Aryan sat beside the sage.

"Rishi," Aryan began, "I've studied black holes and quantum gates, but the more I read the Mahabharata, the less it feels like fiction. It's too… calculated. Too exact. Could it be a record of a lost civilisation's final war?"

Rishi smiled, stirring the fire. "To the poet, a tale. To the mystic, a lesson. To the scientist? A forgotten manual."

Aryan leaned forward. "Arjuna didn't just *receive* divine weapons—he acquired knowledge, underwent training, and passed tests. The Brahmastra, Pashupatastra… these were technologies, weren't they?"

"Indeed," said Rishi. "They were bound to mantras—vibrational signatures encoded with intention and mental alignment. You'd call it biometric encryption or quantum authentication."

"And Krishna?" Aryan asked.

"Ah," Rishi chuckled, "Krishna was the ultimate polymath. He could dilate time, collapse wave functions, and run entire simulations within minds. That scene where he reveals the Virat Roop to Arjuna—it wasn't a metaphor. It was controlled neural immersion. Like a quantum VR, where timelines unfold and collapse at once."

Aryan was nearly breathless. "The battlefield feed to the blind king through Sanjaya… that's telemetry! Real-time war analytics. And the Pushpaka Vimana—clearly an anti-gravity vehicle!"

"But why was all of it lost?" he asked, now frowning. "Why are there no remnants?"

Rishi's face turned grave. "Because when Brahmastras clashed, they did not just destroy armies—they fractured the biosphere. The land cracked. Skies burned. Survivors hid underground. The knowledge was sealed. Those who remembered feared its return."

Aryan whispered, "So the rituals we now perform... they're degraded versions of those protocols?"

Rishi nodded. "Symbols stripped of function. Like pressing buttons on a broken remote."

Aryan sat in silence, the campfire throwing strange shadows. "We're re-inventing the same wheel. Missiles, AI, drones… all echoes."

"Knowledge," Rishi said, "is a spiral. What once was, shall be again."

Then Rishi went on, with stories buried deeper still:

"Bhishma," he said, "knew regenerative nanomedicine. When wounded, his prana could be slowed to near stasis. He lay on that bed of arrows by invoking somatic stasis protocol, a consciousness-driven technology, exactly like induced cryostasis. And do you recall Arjuna creating a spring of water to quench Bhishma's thirst? He used a localised hydrokinetic tool embedded in his celestial bow. It was programmed to detect sub-surface aquifers and draw them up with minimal displacement."

"And Dronacharya?" Aryan prompted.

"A pioneer in sentient combat AI," Rishi replied. "His instruction to Arjuna was never about archery—it was about predictive modelling and meditation that synced brainwaves with targeting algorithms. When he meditated to become undefeatable, it was not spiritual escape—it was synchronising his neural system with battlefield analytics."

The more Aryan heard, the more the myths dissolved into equations and engineering marvels. Not magic, not miracle—just forgotten science.

The next morning, as the fog lifted and GPS signals returned, the group thanked the sage, only to find him missing—no footprints, no sign of departure. Just the faint scent of sandalwood in the breeze.

As they trekked back toward civilisation, Aryan turned to his colleague and said, "You know… that man might've been Krishna himself."

His friend laughed. "What makes you say that?"

Aryan smiled. "He left me with a thought. That there's a reason the word *science* lives inside *conscience*. What we *can* do must always be tempered by what we *should* do."

As the Himalayan wind carried away the last smoke trails of the campfire, the team descended, unaware that they'd just been gifted a revelation straddling the sacred and the scientific.

End of Book